NOTHIN' SHORT OF DYIN'

JOHN R. RIGGS

authorHOUSE®

AuthorHouse™
1663 Liberty Drive
Bloomington, IN 47403
www.authorhouse.com
Phone: 1-800-839-8640

First published by AuthorHouse 05/31/2011

ISBN: 978-1-4567-5030-5 (sc)
ISBN: 978-1-4567-5031-2 (e)

Printed in the United States of America

There's nothin' short of dyin'
Half as lonesome as the sound
On a sleeping city sidewalk
Sunday morning coming down.

From the song,
"Sunday Morning Coming Down"

CHAPTER 1

November is not a nice month in Wisconsin. It starts with rain and ends in snow. Usually there is no sunrise, no sunset—only one long gray litany of clouds that barely brightens as the day wears on, then falls to dusk again. November is the trough between October and December, Halloween and Christmas, the icy ankle-deep slush that you trudge through on the way to your first cold of the season. And if Thanksgiving just happens to fall somewhere toward its end, well, that's appropriate. Thank God, you say. It's almost over.

All of which belied this, the clearest bluest of days in mid-November. I knew it couldn't last. Besides, it was Monday. "Monday, Monday, can't trust that day."

I am Garth Ryland, owner and editor of the *Oakalla Reporter*, a small weekly newspaper, and the author of a syndicated column that in the past few years has grown beyond the borders of Wisconsin into the neighboring states. I live and work in Oakalla, a small self-contained, self-satisfied town, with its own school, bank, cheese plant, drugstore, hardware, and five-and-dime; its own Centennial Community Park and Corner Bar and Grill, good guys and bad guys, heartthrobs and curmudgeons, self-starters and self-righteous, peculiar to small towns everywhere. We have no Wal-Mart, or any other big box store. We are too small for one, and too contrary, which is the way I like it.

I was standing by my north office window, admiring the coverall inch of powdery snow that had fallen in the night when I saw Cecil Hardwick drive slowly by on Gas Line Road, then make the turn south onto Berry Street. When I heard him pull up and stop outside my office, then the slam of a car door, I sighed and returned to my desk. Five would get me ten that the trouble I'd been expecting had arrived.

"Morning, Cecil," I said as he entered my office through its east door.

"Morning, Garth. I hope I'm not interrupting anything."

"No. I haven't gotten that far yet."

Cecil Hardwick had been Oakalla's town marshal for the past few months, and its only town marshal to date. The job was created to fill the void left when our latest county sheriff resigned. Throughout Oakalla's history, the Adams County Sheriff had always lived in Oakalla and thus looked after its citizens, as well as those in the neighboring townships. But because of the resignation of Sheriff

Wayne Jacoby, and the brief woeful reigns of his two prede-cessors, Whitey Huffer and Harold Clark, the Wisconsin State Police now looked after Adams County, and the town of Oakalla had to look after itself. It wasn't supposed to be that way. Elections should have been held two weeks ago for a new sheriff. However, the County Council had decided to postpone the election for another year, until at least one qualified candidate could be found.

Cecil took off his hat, as was his custom whenever indoors, and stood there looking uncomfortable, as was also his custom whenever he was in my presence. A re-tired dairy farmer, he was a tall lean man with large big-knuckled hands, no hips on which to hang a gun belt, if he had deigned to carry a gun, watery blue eyes that did not lend confidence at first glance, a large round Charlie Brown face, and a thin border of short gray hair around his otherwise bald head. He was dressed in full uniform, which included shirt, tie, pants, and jacket, hat, boots, and badge. His .38 Smith and Wesson Police Special I kept in my top desk drawer in case Cecil ever changed his mind about carrying it.

"I just got a call from Beezer Portnoy," Cecil said. "He says there's a pickup parked in his alfalfa field there along Gas Line Road, and that it's been there all night. He wants me to, in his words, 'get that bucket of bolts to hell out of his field.'"

"Why is that a problem?" I said, not seeing one.

"It's not my jurisdiction. That alfalfa field lies just east of the city limits sign."

The gist of which meant that it was my jurisdiction and hence, my problem, since because of the special deputy badge I carried, I was the only remaining Adams County police officer. The badge had been given to me years ago by then Sheriff Rupert Roberts, and it was out of respect for him that I still carried it.

"Call the state police. They'll take care of it," I said, not wanting to ruin the best day in a fortnight.

"I did. Trooper Higgins said that with all due respect, he would defer to you on this one."

"I'm not surprised." Trooper Michael Higgins was my second all-time favorite lawman, but that didn't stop him from pulling rank at his convenience.

"Beezer said he'd meet us there," Cecil said, as if the issue were settled, which it was.

"Let me get my coat."

A couple minutes later I climbed into Cecil's brown Chevy Impala with the big gold star on each side and the blue-and-white bubble light on top. A couple minutes after that we parked along Gas Line Road at the north edge of Beezer Portnoy's alfalfa field and began walking toward Beezer, who stood between his Moped and a dark-colored pickup, parked about 50 yards into his field. Even though the sun was blinding bright, the wind at my back was cold. I pulled up the fake-fur collar on my sheepherder's coat, jammed my hands into its pockets, and wished I'd worn my stocking cap.

"It's about time you got here," Beezer said to Cecil, as he hugged himself and hopped back and forth from one foot to the other. "I'm 30 seconds shy of freezing both my big toes."

"Why didn't you get in the truck if you were cold?" Cecil said.

"Because it ain't my truck to get into."

Beezer was a lifelong bachelor ("always have been, always will be"), who had bought Josh Henry's place at a sheriff's sale several years ago. Formerly he'd lived in far northeastern Adams County in a log cabin that he'd built himself from native timbers and that had neither an inside toilet nor running water. What it did have, however, was a section of woods surrounding it, plenty of game in the woods to hunt and trap, an abundance of wild plants and roots to eat in season and/or dry for the winter, and a small cold-water trout stream running through it. Beezer probably would have been there yet if he and Amos Fullford, the owner of the land, hadn't had a falling out over whose right it was to say who could hunt and fish there, and who couldn't.

So after his forced eviction, Beezer dug up what proved to be a considerable stash of money, bought Josh Henry's cabin and the surrounding 160 acre farm of mostly hills and hollows, scrub oak and pine barrens, took his ten boxes of books and a garbage bag full of clothes, and "moved to town," even though his nearest neighbor, Hattie Peeler, lived a half mile away. His one fertile field, the one in which we were then standing, he kept in alfalfa year after year to feed the herd of deer that had the run of the place. The fattest deer in

Adams County, and because Beezer no longer hunted, the most available, they were a magnet for many of the local hunters, who took it as a personal challenge to get one of "Beezer's deer." As a result, Beezer was forever patrolling his property during deer season, trying to keep the hunters out.

The pickup, I judged, belonged to one of them, who, for whatever reason, was foolish enough to park it there in the first place and then brazen enough to leave it overnight. Either that or he had managed to shoot himself and now lay dead in the woods—a thought that, despite its sweet irony, didn't necessarily please me.

Still doing his tap dance with his gray wool stocking cap pulled down to the bridge of his nose and a malevolent glare in his yellow gamecock eyes, Beezer reminded me of a bantam rooster about to sink his spurs into someone. "So what are you two yahoos going to do about that truck?" he said.

"You mind if we take a look at it first?" I said. "Then we'll decide what to do with it."

Beezer's brows were furrowed, the work knots on his hands poking like extra knuckles through the skin. Now in his early 70s, he had weathered the years like hardwood, growing ever grayer, more deeply grained.

"Just don't take all day," he said. "But I can tell you right now that truck ain't from around here. Go around front and have a gander at the plates, you don't believe me."

Cecil followed me around to the front of the truck where we discovered a Confederate flag in the shape of a license plate. There was no other license plate visible, either front or back.

"I don't like the looks of this," Cecil said.

"Welcome aboard, Cecil."

The truck itself, a 15 year old Ford F150, was in color somewhere between purple and black—that fevered shade of summer sky born in the stillness right before the storm. Caked with red mud front to back, it had one of its headlights broken, what appeared to be a bullet hole on the passenger's side of the windshield, another bullet hole in the driver's door, and when I opened that door, what appeared to be a smear of blood on the brown plastic seat. Examining the broken headlight, Cecil discovered what he estimated to be a .45 slug lying amidst the fragments of broken glass. I dug another slug out of the front seat.

I tried to give my slug to Cecil at the same time that he tried to give his to me. Neither one of us wanted to be the officer in charge.

"Well, what's the verdict?" Beezer said, peering over my shoulder to look at the slugs. "Am I right or not?"

"Is there more to this story?" I said to him.

"Might be."

"You mind telling it to me?"

"As long as we're inside where it's warm."

"We'll meet you back at Cecil's car."

Beezer kick-started his Moped and took off in high gear toward the Impala. He had been driving the Moped to and from town twice a day ever since last summer, when after bending his elbow one too many times at the Corner Bar and Grill, he'd missed the turn at Perrin Street and Gas Line Road and driven his 1952 Buick Roadmaster through Delpha Wright's lilac hedge, across her yard, and into her willow tree. The Roadmaster, now grounded, was parked in the old barn behind Beezer's cabin. It hadn't been licensed since 1978 and Beezer had never been licensed.

Beezer thought that Cecil, the investigating officer, was being a "hard-ass prick" for not letting him continue to drive the Buick and wasn't shy about voicing his opinion. Cecil told Beezer that he was lucky not to be doing 20 to life.

"Your thoughts on the subject?" Cecil said, as we watched Beezer jump the ditch, careen out of control, and nearly collide with the Impala before he laid the Moped down amidst a shower of snow.

"You should have insisted on a tricycle."

"I mean about the pickup."

Beezer got to his feet and brushed himself off before climbing into the back seat of the Impala.

"I think the less said the better, until we can get a handle on things," I said.

"What about Beezer? You going to warn him off?"

"Not if we can find some other way to keep him quiet."

We joined Beezer in the Impala, which with the sun pouring in was toasty warm and smelled like Beezer. Not a necessarily unpleasant odor, its gaminess reminded me of my rabbit-hunting days with the Scooners back in

Indiana, when we'd pile four of us into the front seat of a pickup and drive to the nearest brier patch. You wouldn't want to wear it to the opera, but around a campfire, with road kill on the spit, it would suit just fine.

"It's hot in here," Beezer said, unzipping his coveralls.

"That's what you wanted," Cecil answered, turning the key to on so that he could roll down his window.

"If it weren't for you, I'd have my own car to sit in," Beezer said.

"If it weren't for you, Delpha Wright would still have her willow tree and ten years on her life."

I gave Cecil a look that said I'd been down this road with Beezer before and didn't intend to travel it again. "Beezer, when did you first notice that pickup in your alfalfa field?" I said.

Deliberately ignoring Cecil, Beezer turned and spoke directly to me. "On my way home from the Corner Bar and Grill last evening. As you might know, I take my breakfast and supper there. Lunch, such as it is, I eat at home."

"What did you do once you saw the pickup there?"

"Hid my Moped in the ditch and tried to wait them out."

"Them?"

"Whoever was back there deer hunting. I figured they were trying to take a crack at Old Elmo while I was off to supper."

According to Beezer, Old Elmo was the biggest

baddest buck in Adams County. Local hunters, fired by Beezer's description, had been trying for years, in vain, to kill him. Either Old Elmo was too smart for them, Beezer too good at protecting Old Elmo, or he was another one of Beezer's tall tales, for which Beezer was noted.

"I take it you had no luck waiting them out," I said.

"Not a whit. I stayed until the snow started to fall in earnest, then hopped on my Moped and drove home. I was out there at first light again, but they didn't show then either, so I came on into town for breakfast and once I'd finished, called what's his name here." He continued to ignore Cecil. "Would have called you, Garth, if I'd known you were still in the business."

"I'm not here by choice. Believe me. So do me a favor, will you, and sit on this for a while until I get my bearings."

"I'll sit on it as long as you like, you get that truck out of my field."

"I'll talk to Danny Palmer on my way to lunch. Is that soon enough?"

"Suits me if it suits you. I'll be on my way now."

Beezer climbed out of the back seat of the Impala and onto his Moped, and headed home.

"Well?" Cecil said, as we watched Beezer scatter a flock of crows that were feeding in the picked corn field next to the road.

"Not deer hunters."

"I sort of figured that. Who is it, then?"

I wished I knew.

CHAPTER 2

Hattie Peeler was a full-blooded Chippewa, who had lived nearly all of her 90 plus years in Oakalla, over half of them in the same house in which she lived now. Brown, wiry, tough as rawhide, and about as forgiving, she had luminous black eyes that could bore a hole right through you without even trying and a way of making her point without ever saying a word.

Hattie lived south of Gas Line Road in the last house east before the city limits sign. Hers was a two-story, green-roofed, white frame house with wide windows, black shutters, three gables, and a red brick chimney. Surrounded by sugar maples, widely spaced so that no two tops touched, the house was pleasantly cool throughout the summer, but airy and bright, which gave it the flavor of woods without the isolation. Once fall came, the trees turned red, yellow, and my favorite, an almost neon orange. And once the leaves fell, the house was bathed in sunshine, when there was sunshine, winter to spring.

I climbed the three wooden steps to Hattie's front porch and knocked on her storm door. To the west was Centennial Park. To the east was the alfalfa field where the Ford F150 sat. In my pocket were the two slugs that were starting to weigh me down.

Hattie opened the door after my third knock and stood squinting at me, as if the sunlight were hurting her eyes. Or maybe she didn't recognize me. It had been years since we'd last talked.

"Garth Ryland," she said at last. "I might have known."

"Known what, Hattie?"

"That there was trouble afoot."

She stepped out onto the front porch, wearing a doe-skin dress and moccasins. Long-sleeved and beaded with a high neck, the dress hung almost to the floor of the porch, while Hattie's thick silky white hair, which she normally wore in braids, hung loosely down to her waist and gave her face a softness that it normally didn't have.

"How would you know there's trouble afoot?" I said.

She nodded in the direction of the pickup. "I saw you over there earlier. You and the marshal both. I can see almost like I used to, now that those cataracts are off my eyes."

"You happen to see who was in the pickup?"

"No. Heard them come in, though. About six last night, I think it was. Thought for sure it was somebody after Old Elmo. But when it was still there this morning, I knew that couldn't be the case."

Hattie's eyes had started to water in the bright sunlight. She reached into the pocket of her dress and pulled out a pair of Polaroid sunglasses and put them on. They made her look like an ancient gun moll, who had buried as many men as secrets.

"Then there really is an Old Elmo?" I said.

"Beezer claims there is."

"Beezer claims a lot of things that are open to question."

"I suppose so," she said, neither agreeing nor disagreeing.

I waited a few seconds to see if she would volunteer anything else. When she didn't, I said, "I like your dress. I don't think I've ever seen you wear it before."

Hattie took off her sunglasses, and holding out her arms, took a long look at the dress herself. "It was my wedding dress. I'm counting on it being my burial dress when the time comes."

"I hope that's not any time soon."

"Soon enough, I imagine," she said without regret. "Every day after 80's a gift, and every day after 90's a curse. I don't plan on seeing a 100." She put her sunglasses back in her pocket, went inside, and closed the door.

I walked on to my office, spent a couple hours calling my sources and gathering the news for that week's edition of the *Oakalla Reporter*, then walked to the Marathon service station. I might have driven, had I not liked to walk. Had I not owned a car that made walking anywhere within a radius of a mile or two seem the lesser of two evils. Danny Palmer, owner of the Marathon, Oakalla's volunteer fire chief, ace mechanic, family man, and all around good guy, was inside working on his wrecker, as Sniffy Smith, my "Friday only" barber now that he was retired, watched the drive for Danny from his favorite perch atop a gray metal stool.

A small, soft, solemn man, Sniffy had the habit of sniffing loudly whenever excited, hence his nickname. Since he now spent most of his days loafing at the Marathon, Danny put him to work watching the drive whenever Danny was away on a wrecker call or busy doing something else, as he was today. What Danny failed to realize, or chose to ignore, was that Sniffy's eagle-eye attention to the drive was a ruse. When alone at the Marathon, Sniffy hid at the first sign that the customer on the drive was coming in after him to have him pump the gas. Usually he made good his escape—except for Ruth Krammes, my housekeeper, and Beulah Peters, Ruth's nemesis, who were unparalleled in their ability to find Sniffy's hiding place and read him the riot act as they dragged him out to the pumps. It wasn't that Ruth or Beulah couldn't pump the gas herself. As Ruth explained it to me, she "wouldn't give the little twerp the satisfaction of getting away with it." And if Beulah were polled, I imagined that she would give a similar answer.

"How's it going?" I said to Danny, knowing that

he'd spent most of the weekend rebuilding the wrecker's transmission.

He wheeled his cart out from under the wrecker. "I'm hoping to be done tonight. Why? You need it?"

"Beezer does. There's a pickup parked in his alfalfa field that needs towing."

Danny took a clean rag from the pile on his workbench to wipe his hands. "Tomorrow morning will probably be the earliest that I can get to it."

"I'll tell Beezer to sit tight, then."

Sniffy gave a loud sniff of indignation. He hated to be ignored. "What pickup you talking about, Garth?"

"There's a purple-black pickup with a Confederate flag on the front of it parked in Beezer's alfalfa field. It's been there all night. Beezer wants it out of there."

Sniffy gave another loud sniff, then straightened and leaned forward as if he were about to strike a track. "Wish I'd known that earlier. There was a man in here looking for that very truck."

"How long ago?"

"About an hour, I'd say." He looked at Danny, who nodded in agreement.

"Did he say why he was looking for it?" I said.

"Nope. He just said he was looking for it. Then when we told him we hadn't seen it, he asked where there was a good place to eat in town and where he might be able to get a room on short notice. I told him the Corner Bar and Grill was the best, and only, place to eat in town, and that Beulah Peters sometimes took in boarders."

15

"What did the man look like?"

"Big man. Not real tall, but solid. He'd go 220 at least, and not an ounce of it fat. Brown hair, sort of grayish colored eyes, and about 30, wouldn't you say, Danny? And he walked with a limp."

"What was he wearing?"

"Jeans and a brown leather jacket. Real leather, too, it looked like to me."

"Anything else you remember about him?"

As Sniffy thought it over, Danny said, "He spoke with a southern accent. Deep South would be my guess. And he was driving a white Grand Am with Louisiana plates. It looked like a rental to me."

"He must have made quite an impression on you both. Since you remember him so well," I said.

Sniffy and Danny exchanged glances. Then Danny attached his impact wrench to the air hose, a socket to the wrench, and wheeled back under the wrecker.

"You tell him, Sniffy," Danny said.

"Tell him what?"

"What you told me."

Sniffy rocked forward and back on his stool a couple times then said, "I told Danny, there goes a dangerous man. Polite as can be, and soft spoken, but eyes as hard and cold as a crick rock. It wouldn't do to be standing between him and anything he wanted."

I left the Marathon and started uptown. I was still a half block from the Corner Bar and Grill when I saw a large man in a brown leather jacket limp across Jackson

Street, get into a white late-model car with out-of-state plates and drive as far as the four-way stop, where he turned left. He could have been on his way to Beulah Peters' house, which was three blocks south on School Street, but I had no way of knowing, and no reason yet to find out.

Inside the Corner Bar and Grill it was quiet for a lunch crowd. I took my customary stool at the counter and ordered the day's special of Beef Manhattan from Bernice, the owner and noon waitress.

"And applesauce on the side," I said as I put the menu back in the chrome rack there on the counter.

Behind me, all four booths along the north wall were full, but no one was saying much, and if he spoke at all, he spoke quietly to the person across from him. Except for the stool on my immediate left the counter was also full, but no one there was saying much either. Even the barroom was quiet. Nothing playing on the juke box. Nobody throwing darts or pitching pennies or carrying somebody high over a lost wager. Only the flick of a lighter and the clink of someone's glass against the bar.

"Did somebody die?" I asked Bernice when she brought me my lunch.

"Not that I know of."

"Then why is it so quiet in here today?"

"Strangers sometimes do that."

Now in her 60s, Bernice had run the Corner Bar and Grill with the help of Hiram, the bartender, ever since her husband died 20 years earlier. In the time I'd known

17

her, I'd seen her glasses go from black plastic to gold wire frames, and her hair go from brown to gray to blond, but little else about her had changed. She was one of the constants in life we would take for granted, until she was no longer there.

"You mean the guy that left right before I came in?" I said.

"Yes. He was in here asking if anyone had seen a dark colored pickup with a Confederate flag on the front."

"Had anyone?"

"Not that I know of. Of course, Beezer was in here at breakfast, asking me if I knew who owned such a truck. But I didn't volunteer that information."

"Any particular reason why not?"

"None of his business, I figured. He'll find out soon enough anyway. Oakalla can't keep a secret long."

"Do you know where he was headed from here?"

"He asked where Beulah Peters lived. I told him."

"He happen to tell you his name?"

"No. And I didn't ask." She refilled my water glass. "Who is he anyway, Garth?"

"I have no idea."

"And the pickup he's looking for?"

"The last time I saw it, it was in Beezer's alfalfa field. By morning, it should be at the Marathon."

"It shouldn't be hard for him to find it there."

"I wouldn't think so."

After lunch I walked back down Gas Line Road to the long low white concrete block building that housed the

Oakalla Reporter, where I went to work calling all of my sources that I hadn't called that morning, or who hadn't called me. The survival of any small town newspaper like mine depended on the pieces, those minute, often tedious details that were someone's life. Put all together they might become a mosaic, a larger whole for one to study and ponder if, like me, one were so inclined. But that's not why most people bought and read my paper. They bought it to see whose name might be there, perhaps their own, and who had died and who had married and who had gone away for the winter, and to where. They couldn't read about those things in the *Madison Capital Times* or the *Chicago Tribune*, and they surely wouldn't be seeing them on CNN. They could read about it in blogs and e-mails on the internet, but seeing it on the internet wasn't the same as seeing it in print. For lack of a better explanation, I was the clearinghouse of gossip.

So it was my job to gather the news of Oakalla, trivial as it might be, and report it week in and week out. In my column, I could offer my opinion on whatever I wanted. But that's not what paid the rent.

On my bad days I might chafe at the bit, wishing that there were something larger at stake and that I were a larger player in it. Yet on the whole I liked my job. Not just because I was good at it, or because I was a big fish in a small puddle, but because I really did care about Oakalla and its people, and because there was always the hope, fragile though it might be, that what I did made my corner of the world a little bit better.

———————

At five, I closed up shop and went home to find Ruth still wearing her coat and scarf and in the process of sorting our mail.

"Here," she said, throwing a letter down on the kitchen table in front of me.

Ruth is a tall, big-boned Swede somewhere in her 70s. We have been together well over a decade and although her once blond hair is a little grayer, her always bold step a little slower than when we first met, she has not lost one drop of her passion for life, or her impatience with fools, or her willingness to bet it all on one roll of the dice.

We don't always get along. Neither do we always agree, particularly when the subject is the best way for me to live my life. But we count on each other to help us through the hard times. That failing, we always know whom to blame.

I let the letter lie where it had fallen. Though the writing was familiar, I didn't know any Dieters from New Mexico.

"Are you going to open it?" Ruth said.

"In a minute. How are things at the shelter?"

"Quiet. The way I like them."

Ruth worked from eight to five at the new shelter for abused women that occupied the house where the late Dr. William T. Airhart and then his niece, Dr. Abby Airhart, now a resident in pathology at Henry Ford Hospital in Detroit, used to live. The shelter had nearly cost me my happy home. I had opposed it from the day that Abby put Ruth in charge of its remodeling, until it opened its doors a couple months ago, which had put me at odds with both Abby and Ruth. But now that it was a fact and I more or less had Ruth back again, she and I had made peace and moved on. Jerry Lewis has said that he likes progress, but hates change. I felt that way about the shelter. I would never like what they have done to Doc's house, which had been my home away from home, but I couldn't fault their reasons or their results.

Ruth took the letter from the table, opened it with a paring knife, and handed it to me. "You know who it's from, don't you?" I said.

"No. But I have my hopes."

I read the letter. It was from Diana Baldwin, Diana Dieter now. She had married Gerald, the rancher, in October. I handed the letter to Ruth to read.

"So what are you going to do about it?" Ruth said, handing the letter back to me.

"Send her my congratulations."

"Without regret?"

I went to the kitchen cabinet to fix me an Old Crow and ginger ale. I sometimes did my best reflecting slightly under the influence.

"I don't know, Ruth. There's a song from the 70s, 'MacArthur's Park.' Whenever I hear it, I think of Diana."

"I'm not familiar with it."

I gave the letter a toss, watched it skip off the table and onto the floor. "Just as well, I suppose."

"I thought you were over her."

"I am. Have been for quite a while. But you know, another time, another place, we could have made it."

"So you say. But you had your time and place, and you didn't make it. That should tell you something."

I took a drink of my Old Crow and ginger ale. It felt good going down. "Beezer Portnoy has a F150 pickup parked in his alfalfa field. It's been there since last evening. There's a stranger in town looking for that selfsame pickup," I said.

Ruth went to the hall closet to hang up her coat and scarf. "That's news to me. Who told you about it?"

"Cecil Hardwick by way of Beezer." I took the two slugs out of my pocket and laid them on the table. "We also found these in the pickup with a smear of what looked like blood on the seat."

Ruth gave the slugs a cursory glance and headed for the stove, where she began pulling out pots and pans in preparation for supper. "There could be a simple explanation for all of it," she said.

"That's what I'm hoping."

"Except there's a stranger in town, you said."

"Yes."

"Where from?"

"He's driving a white rental car with Louisiana plates. Or so Danny Palmer says."

Ruth had found the pots and pans she needed and closed the door on the rest of them. "That's a long way to come looking for a pickup truck."

"My thoughts exactly."

"How did you get involved? I thought you intended to let Cecil handle things from now on."

"It was Cecil's idea. The truck's outside the city limits. It's the county's jurisdiction. Or the state's. But the state passed it on to me."

Ruth had three burners lighted and a skillet or pan on each one. I was glad for that because I was hungry and growing hungrier by the minute.

"What are you going to do about the truck? Really going to do about it?" she said.

"Leave it there another night and hope it goes away."

"And if it doesn't?"

"I'll have Danny tow it in tomorrow morning. I've already made arrangements with him."

"To what end?"

"I haven't gotten that far yet."

"You want my advice, Garth, I'd have Danny tow it out to Hidden Quarry and drop it in there. Then you can be sure it won't come back to haunt you."

"It's too late for that, Ruth. It's already haunting me. I'm having a hard time thinking about anything else."

"God help us all, then."

CHAPTER 3

When the fire siren rang in the night, I was already awake. A light sleeper, even on the best of nights, I'd just had a dream about Minnesota. I was trying to get to Red Horse Lake in my canoe, but all these houses with black pickups parked outside kept blocking my way until I finally gave up, parked my canoe, and began bobber fishing from shore. But try though I might, I couldn't get my bait in the water. Then my eyes opened, and a few seconds later, the siren went off.

I dressed and went downstairs, where Ruth stood at the kitchen window in her antebellum pink flowered robe and the fur-lined moccasins that I'd bought for her many Christmases ago. Had I not known better, seeing her mussed hair and ratty robe, I would have thought she'd just crawled out of her cardboard box and come in off the street.

"Have you called to find out where the fire is?" I said.

"Fickle Store."

I groaned. Fickle Store was at least five miles south of town.

"Better there than somebody's house," she said.

I took my coat out of the hall closet, but before I could make my way to the garage, I saw someone pull up out front and flash his headlights.

"Cecil?" I said.

"Be my guess."

"Don't wait up for me," I said, knowing that she would

Cecil and I neither one spoke until we were well out of town on Fickle Road. It was a still, moonlit night, the stars scattered and dim, yesterday's snow, partially melted by an all-day sun, a patchwork quilt of woods and barn lots and snow ghosts on the north-facing hills. Already we could see a dome of fire to the south. From a distance, fire can look like city lights and city lights can look like fire. It all depends on your perspective, what you think your eyes see.

"From here it looks like Fickle Store is already a goner," Cecil said.

"From here, too. Who called in the fire?"

"Jasper did."

Jasper was Jasper Peterson, the owner of Fickle Store.

"How long ago?" I said.

"About a minute before the fire siren rang."

For the fire to have already broken through the roof, it must have been burning for some time before Jasper called. "What time is it anyway?" I said. The battery had died in my watch and I'd not yet replaced it.

25

Cecil looked at the car's clock. "Midnight. The witching hour."

"Figures."

Fickle Store was indeed a goner when we arrived. Fire had eaten through the roof in several places, engulfed a nearby stand of cedars, and was showering sparks on Jasper Peterson's house fifty yards away. All three trucks from Oakalla were there and at least a dozen volunteer firemen, but the best that they could do, amidst the sparks, the confusing whirl of lights, the growing crowd of onlookers that kept coming and coming, in fact the only thing that they could do, was to knock down the fire to keep it from spreading to Jasper's three gas pumps out front.

Cecil, to his credit, did his best to control the crowd, but he couldn't be everywhere at once, and the firemen were too busy fighting the fire to give him much help. Half of Oakalla and the surrounding countryside seemed to be there, which made me wonder who was minding the store back in town? It seemed that it would have been a great time to rob the bank, or to do anything else you didn't want anyone to witness.

Cecil and I were on our way home. My most vivid memory of the past few hours was the look in Jasper Peterson's eyes as the store buckled under the weight of the roof, then collapsed in a shower of sparks as firemen and spectators alike ran for cover. Up until then, Jasper must have harbored the feeble hope that something somehow could be saved. But when the store collapsed, and that fireball roared up out of its belly like a thing alive, all of Jasper's hope fled, and the look in his eyes was as black as the trampled mud hole that was once his yard.

"There are some days I hate this job," Cecil spoke to me for the first time since we'd left.

"I know the feeling."

"What did all those idiots think they were doing there anyway? It wasn't a goddamn sideshow."

"Curiosity perhaps. But they always come."

"If you burn it, I will come?"

"Something like that."

"Makes me sad I'm part of the human race."

"Give yourself a day or two. You'll get over it."

The next couple miles passed in silence. Then Cecil said, "What's your take on the fire?"

"I don't know. I'll have to talk to Danny."

Danny Palmer and one truck and crew were still at the fire and probably would remain there for at least another hour, before going home and cleaning up just in time to go to work. Being a volunteer fireman was a thankless job, but a most necessary one. And at least you got free seconds at all the fish fries you served.

"Do you think the fire has anything to do with that pickup parked in Beezer's alfalfa field?" Cecil said.

"I don't see how, Cecil. That's quite a stretch, even for me."

"Then answer me this question. Why is it still sitting there? Beezer called me again on it this evening."

"I didn't think Beezer had a phone."

"He doesn't. He caught me at the Corner Bar and Grill."

"To answer your question, Danny's wrecker is down. He hopes to have it fixed today, but with the fire, I don't know. I was supposed to tell Beezer, but forgot."

"Something else on your mind?" For someone who sometimes didn't seem to have a clue, Cecil could turn circumspect at the most awkward times.

"Diana Baldwin got married again. She wrote to let me know."

"Weren't you two once an item?"

"Yes. A long time ago." We were coming into Oakalla. I'd be home soon. "The funny thing is, Cecil, I don't miss her nearly as much as the good times we once had together. It didn't seem so strange then to think that they might last."

When he didn't answer right away, I thought that maybe I'd overshot him. Then he said, "Speaking as a man who's been married to the same woman since he was 18, the good times never last. They might get better, they might get worse, but they don't last. Not in the way we want them to. Not in the way that can keep us at the same sweet moment all our lives. Only memory can do that. And to my mind, that's what memory is for. To re-mind that old fart I see in the mirror every morning that he once had what it took to do whatever needed doing, and that it's still in there somewhere, though God knows where."

"You've thought about this before," I said.

"About every other day."

———————

At home the front porch light was on, as was the kitchen light and the pole lamp beside my chair in the living room. Ruth, however, was conspicuous by her absence.

"Ruth, you here?" I called up the stairs.

When she didn't answer, I went up the stairs to her bedroom and looked in to see that it was empty. So I went to bed. A couple hours later my radio alarm clock came on the very second I finally drifted off to sleep.

I walked down the hall to find Ruth's bed still empty and Ruth nowhere in sight. In the past I would have been worried, but with the shelter now in operation it was likely that she was there, since battered women don't usually have an array of options as to when they leave home. I left her a note saying that I would be eating breakfast at the Corner Bar and Grill. We'd sort things out when I got home that evening.

Beezer was already there when I arrived at the Corner Bar and Grill. I knew that for a fact the moment I saw his Moped parked outside the front door.

Inside, Beezer, Bernice, and I had the place to ourselves. But it was early yet. By eight the place would be packed with customers—if for no other reason than to discuss last night's fire. Yesterday's blue coveralls shucked down to his waist, Beezer sat on his favorite stool there at the lunch counter with scrambled egg on his lip and the tops of his long underwear showing. I took the stool beside him.

"Where was the fire last night?" Beezer said.

"Fickle Store."

"Heard the siren go off. But when the trucks kept going south out of town, I figured it wasn't worth it to me to try to get there. Not on a motor scooter, leastwise."

Scrambled eggs looked good to me, so I ordered some along with bacon, whole wheat toast, a cup of coffee, and a small glass of orange juice. Hash browns would have gone well with the rest of it, but you have to draw the line somewhere. And if my conscience still bothered me, I'd leave the jelly off the toast.

Beezer said, "I want to thank you for getting rid of that pickup. It was starting to grow roots."

"You mean it's gone?"

"As far as I can tell. It was gone this morning when I drove by. Good thing, too, because I was about to take matters into my own hands."

"Danny must have gone after it after he got home from the fire," I said, thinking aloud.

"Whatever the case, I'm glad of it. I didn't like the feeling it gave out. Didn't like it at all." As if to prove his point, he put his arms back inside his coveralls and zipped them all the way up.

"What feeling was that, Beezer?"

"Like it was possessed or something. You tell me. What kind of person drives a truck like that, one headlight, no license plate, and the color of a storm cloud? Then parks it in a field and disappears, poof! Just like that. Nobody I'd want sleeping at the foot of my bed, I don't think."

At Beezer's poof! I jumped a little. So did Bernice who was setting down my cup of coffee.

"Thanks, Beezer," she said as she wiped coffee off the counter. "That's just what I needed to start my day off right."

"Better than a sharp stick in the eye," he replied.

"Don't tempt me," she said on her way back to the kitchen.

———

By the time I finished breakfast the place had started to fill up, and as I expected, most of the talk was about the fire, those who had been there armed with what they'd seen, telling those who hadn't been there that what they'd heard was all wrong. I followed Beezer out the door before somebody could corner me.

"Want a ride? I'm heading that way," Beezer said.

It was an offer I couldn't refuse.

Heading down Gas Line Road on the back of Beezer's Moped, my eyes watering, fingers and toes numb from the cold, and my arms tightly wrapped around Beezer's waist, I thought, if only Ruth could see me now. Too grateful for words when Beezer came to a sliding stop in the limestone drive outside my office, I patted the seat and waved him on. Mr. Toad, I thought, as he whipped around the corner without looking or stopping and headed for home. All he needed was a pair of goggles.

Watching him, though, I was soon caught up in one of the most spectacular sunrises I had ever seen. Buried within the lavender bank of clouds in the east was the blood red eye of the sun, its brows laced with molten rivers of light. Above the clouds was an ethereal pane of robin-egg sky, fading even as I watched, and above it a large swath of dress blue sky, topped with a feather of orange smoke. And then there was Beezer, riding straight into it—a speck on the sun, and then a speck no more.

CHAPTER 4

The first thing I did when I got to my office was to call the shelter. Although I didn't feel anxious, I still breathed a sigh of relief when Ruth answered the phone. "Good. It's you," I said.

"Where are you?"

"At my office. When you weren't there when I got home last night and then again this morning, I got a little worried."

"Liddy Bennett called shortly after you left. We had an emergency here at the shelter."

"What sort of emergency?"

"The usual. Nothing that we couldn't handle."

"Will you be home for supper?"

"I don't see why not."

"I'll see you then," I said.

My next call was to Detroit, where Abby answered on the third ring. Two for two. Maybe this was my lucky day.

"Garth?" she said, sounding sleepy. "How do I rate a call so early in the day?"

"Diana got married. I thought you might want to know."

There was a long pause while she processed that information. "How do you feel about that?"

"Glad that it wasn't you."

"There's no danger of that, is there, since I'm madly in love with some dinosaur from Wisconsin."

I loved to hear her voice. It was life itself. "Anyone I know?"

"Maybe. Now, how are you really?"

"Over the hump, I think."

"Because of last spring?" Her voice lost most of its luster.

The past spring there had been a chapter in our lives that could have been the end of us. Because it hadn't been the end of us, it gave me hope for the future.

"Last spring is only part of it," I said. "I think by now I realize that if we can survive being apart for this long, we might survive the duration, however long that is. And who knows, you might still come back to Oakalla."

"I might at that. I've been giving it some thought."

"And?"

"When I know, you'll know."

"Sounds fair enough."

I glanced out my window and saw that the blue sky was retreating to the east ahead of an advancing white shroud. Soon, it seemed, it would be pushed all the way to the horizon.

"Well, I'd better get to work. It's great to hear your voice," I said.

"Same here. You sound better than you have for months."

"Just hold on to that thought about coming back to Oakalla."

"I will. But even at the earliest, it still won't be for another year or so."

"That's a whole lot sooner than I'd been counting on."

"Never, you were thinking?"

"Sad to say."

"Same here."

"What changed your mind?"

"You did. I absolutely cannot bear the thought of you being with anyone else. So I made some inquiries and . . . Well, who knows?"

"I'm hanging up now on that happy thought."

"Love you."

"Yeah. Same here. A whole bunch."

Let it rain, I thought after hanging up. The way I feel now, I might run naked through it.

Then I heard a car door slam, followed shortly by the bang of the storm door on the east side of the building. Reality was about to come calling.

"You have time to take a ride with me?" Cecil said on entering my office.

"Where?"

"Fickle. I'd like for you to be there when I talk to Jasper Peterson."

"About what?"

"His fire last night. Danny is 99 percent sure that it was arson."

"Who'd want to burn down Fickle Store?"

"That's what we need to talk to Jasper about."

"You're not worried about it being out of your jurisdiction?"

Cecil's watery blue eyes were as resolute as I'd ever seen them. "That's why you're coming along."

"Let me get my coat."

The clouds began to gray and thicken on our way to Fickle, as the rain predicted for that afternoon seemed bent on an early arrival. Neither Cecil nor I had spoken to each other since we'd left Oakalla. He was deep in his own thoughts. I was deep in mine.

Fickle, as I remembered it from my boyhood, used to have Fickle Store, a smattering of houses, a church, and a welding shop. Grandmother Ryland and I had stopped there a handful of times during our trips about Adams County. At Fickle Store, to buy me a cream soda and her a sack of horehounds; at the church, to deliver flowers for a friend of hers; and once at the welding shop, to have our muffler fixed after banging our way over the old railroad crossing north of town.

Our trips had for the most part stopped when I was 12. It was then that I had gotten my paper route back home, and could no longer spend my summers with Grandmother. When I moved to Oakalla some 25 years later, only Fickle Store and the house where Jasper Peterson lived remained in Fickle. Jasper was a widower in his late 50s. Since Fickle Store was rumored to be on its last legs, I doubted that Jasper would rebuild. Which meant that Fickle would now be a one house town.

"You ever wonder how Jasper survived as long as he did?" Cecil said.

We parked along the road a short distance away from what was once Fickle Store, now a heap of blackened ruin, smoldering still, despite the 1,000s of gallons of water dumped on top of it. Worm-like with a thin watery smell, its smoke looked blue against the gray sky.

"Coon Lake," I said, referring to the small resort lake a few miles west on County Road J.

"What about in winter?"

"Gas, I guess. Plus, he sold bait all year round."

Along with gasoline and live bait that included night crawlers, crickets, and minnows, Jasper sold hunting and fishing licenses, deer tags, fishing lures, beer, pop, potato chips, dry goods, and canned goods. You rarely saw more than one car in front of his store at a time, but it was equally rare to drive by and see no car at all.

"He couldn't have made a whole lot at it," Cecil said as we climbed out of the Impala.

"No. But he made a living."

Jasper Peterson stood about five-eight, had thin brown hair, a brown-and-white hairy-caterpillar mustache and a small round pot belly that hung over his belt. He'd lost an eye in Vietnam, his wife to ovarian cancer about five years ago, and communication with most of his family since he'd moved from Florida to Wisconsin 22 years ago.

He'd bought Fickle Store, thought to be on its way out even then, from Ulma Friedrickson, widow of its original owner, put in gas pumps and live bait, and, for several years at least, made a going concern of it. I knew all of this because I'd done a human interest story on Jasper in my paper a couple years back.

Cecil and I walked through ankle deep mud to the back of the store where Jasper stood in his brown slacks and navy blue hooded sweatshirt with his eyes downcast and his hands in his pockets, looking as forlorn as I'd ever seen someone look. The aftermath of a fire was always worse than the fire itself. During the fire there was real drama, a contagion of purpose and excitement, and a large cast of players. The next day, you were alone on stage, left to pick up the pieces and clean up the mess.

"It looks like holy hell, doesn't it?" Jasper was gazing at the ruins. "There's nothing left to do now but take a bulldozer to the whole thing."

"You have insurance, don't you?" Cecil said, tactlessly I thought.

Jasper shrugged, looking up for the first time to gauge Cecil's intent. "Enough to cover my building. Not much more than that. Why?"

Cecil ignored my look of warning as he said, "I was

talking to Danny Palmer earlier this morning. He's almost sure the fire was arson."

"Hell, I could have told him that," Jasper said, seeing the implication and not liking it. "In fact, I did tell him that. My exact words were, 'Somebody set that fire, Danny. You can bet on that.'"

"You have anyone in mind?" I said.

Jasper thought a moment and said, "Been a night earlier, I might have."

"Go on."

Jasper looked up at the sky. Sleet had started to fall and was glazing the mud with a coat of ice. "This might take a while," he said.

"We won't melt," Cecil answered.

Easy for him to say. He had a hat, Jasper had a hood, Garth had a collar that reached only to his ears. I wondered what Cecil had been chewing on that morning to make him so contrary.

Jasper pulled his hood up over his head and said, "Okay. Night before last, I guess it was right around dusk. It's hard to tell time when the day's gray like it is today. This pickup pulled up to the gas pumps in front of the store and just sat there. Well, everybody around here, even the lake crowd, knows it's a pump- your-own deal, so I figured whoever it was for a stranger. But it was close to closing, and I was counting out change for the next day, and I didn't want to be bothered unless I had to. So I just sort of forgot about it, and the next thing I know the pickup's driving away with ten dollars worth of gas they didn't pay for."

"That happen often?" I said, curious.

Jasper reached up to tie the string on his hood so the little ice pellets didn't dribble down his throat as they were mine. "Hardly ever," he said. "The college kids over at the lake sometimes have to ask for credit, which I usually give them, or put all their change together so that they can get home, but the last time I was stiffed on gas, except night before last, was at least a couple years ago, the night that cabin burned down over on Coon Lake."

I remembered the fire, but not much else about the incident. Only that it was late fall and the cabin was vacant at the time.

"What happened then?" I said.

"Same sort of thing. Only this happened after dark and by all rights the pumps should have been shut off for the day. But for some reason I must have overlooked it."

"Convenient," Cecil said.

"You got a bur up your butt about something I did or didn't do?" Jasper said, his one good eye pointed at Cecil. "If so, I'd like to hear it."

"It'll keep. Go on," Cecil said.

"I'm losing interest."

I gave Cecil a look once reserved for Harold Clark, or Clarkie, as he was known to us in Oakalla.

"I'll go sit in the car if you like," Cecil said.

When I didn't answer, Cecil left.

"Do you know what his problem is?" Jasper said,

watching Cecil all the way to the Impala. "Truth be told, Garth, I hardly know the man."

"No. But I can probably find out for you."

Jasper shook his head no. "Don't bother. I likely won't be around here much longer anyway."

"Where are you headed?"

"Florida, I think. I'd like to try to get reacquainted with my family before I lose all touch."

"What will you do?"

"Haven't decided yet. Try to wear out as many beaches as I can, I'm thinking, to start out with."

"Mind if I join you?"

"Not if you can pay your own way."

It was starting to rain. I could see it eating away at the sleet.

"How much they hit you up for that night? Two years ago, when the cabin burned down?" I said.

"Only a couple gallons. You know, what might go in a lawnmower gas can. When the fire broke out later that night, I had to wonder if that's not where the gas had gone, especially since I heard through the grapevine that a burned out gas can had been found in the ruins of the cabin."

"How did you know you'd been robbed, since it happened at night?"

"First thing I do every morning after I open up is to turn on my pumps. When I saw they were already on, that's when I noticed a couple gallons were missing."

"They couldn't have been left from the night before?"

"No. I would've remembered."

41

"You ever tell anybody your suspicions?"

"No. And nobody ever asked. I figured that they figured it was a hopeless cause from the get-go."

"Do you remember the color of the pickup two nights ago?"

"Black, blue-black, purple, somewhere in there."

"Do you remember anything else about it?"

"It only had one headlight. I noticed that when it drove in. I remember saying to myself, there's pididdle." His wan smile showed both our ages. "Like we used to do to steal a kiss when we were dating."

"What about its driver?"

"Never saw him. The pump was blocking my view."

"Do you think he intended it that way?"

"As things turned out, yes."

"Do you think he could have returned and set fire to your store last night?"

"He could have, but for the life of me I can't figure out why."

"Maybe he has a grudge against you."

The hard look on Jasper's face said that might be a possibility. "Then you'd better take a look at your new marshal there. He's the only one I know holding a grudge against me."

"And you have no idea why?"

Jasper ignored the question. "I'm getting soaked standing here, Garth. We both are."

He headed for his house. I headed for Cecil's patrol car.

42

CHAPTER 5

"I'm sorry for the way I acted back there, Garth. I've got to learn not to put my personal feelings ahead of my job," Cecil said.

I was back in the Impala, thankful to be out of the rain. "So what gives?" I said.

Cecil put the Impala in gear and backed out into the road. "I'll tell you on the way back to Oakalla."

"I want to take a trip around Coon Lake first."

"Why?"

"Just to see what I might see."

"You're not buying that story about the stolen gas, are you?"

"Jasper said that the pickup was either black, blue-black, or purple, and that it had a headlight out. Have you seen any other pickups lately that fit that description?"

"It doesn't mean a thing. It could all be coincidence."

"That's why we're going to Coon Lake—to find out."

Coon Lake was a small shallow lake of about 500 acres in the shape of a horseshoe, and for the past few years had been used mostly as a party lake by college students and their families. You weren't supposed to water ski on it, or run your boat beyond idle speed, but that was an unwritten rule held over from Coon Lake's earlier, more genteel days, and was violated on a daily basis during the summer by boaters and jet skiers alike. However, the only people that I knew to have drowned there were a man and his daughter, and they were in a rowboat at the time.

"You remember that college student who was killed on his way home from Coon Lake two years ago this past summer?" Cecil said.

He stopped the Impala at the top of the only public boat ramp on Coon Lake. A small public beach to the north of the boat ramp ran along the east shore, but it was sparsely used even in summer, and was deserted today. Out on the lake, gray and still and spotted with rain, a small flock of mallards swam in close formation, quacking quietly among themselves, grousing about either us or the weather.

"I remember the incident. I don't remember the details," I said.

"A car load of kids, none of them the legal age to be drinking, ran off the road and hit a tree when the driver fell asleep at the wheel. Most of them got out with bumps and bruises. My nephew went through the windshield and broke his neck on the tree. They counted a case of beer cans in the car itself. The rest were scattered about the scene. Now, where do you figure they got all that beer?"

I watched as the flock of mallards discreetly put more distance between them and us. No doubt a local flock of Coon Lake mallards, well fed on corn and bread crumbs, they still had to know it was duck hunting season.

"I figure they could have brought it from home. Where do *you* figure they got it?" I said.

"I know where they got it. My other nephew, younger brother to the boy who was killed, was in the car with him. He told me that it had come from Fickle Store, but he wouldn't tell the cops for fear of getting their old buddy, Jasper Peterson, in trouble. None of the kids in the car would."

"Maybe Jasper didn't know they were underage when he sold them the beer," I said.

"That's what IDs are for."

"College students have been known to fake IDs. I once went clear across the country on someone's expired driver's license, drinking in every state."

Cecil shook his head in disagreement. "It's not the first time it's happened. Jasper's been in trouble before for selling booze to minors. He doesn't care what age they are as long as they have the money to pay for it."

"That still doesn't mean he burned his store down for the insurance," I said in Jasper's defense.

"It doesn't mean he didn't either."

We continued along the east shore of Coon Lake, which had summer cabins spaced about every fifty yards or so, with screened in porches that overlooked the lake and long sloping yards of birch, pine, and cottonwood that grew better trees than grass. There among the pines, the rain seemed to have let up for the time being, but that was because it hadn't yet found its way through their tightly knit branches. Out on the lake it continued to pepper down.

We came to an open space surrounded by dead fire-blackened trees, where it was apparent that a cabin had once stood. As we sat in the Impala surveying the scene, I noticed tire tracks in the snow leading into the opening and out again, as if someone had turned around there. I got out of the Impala to take a closer look. Cecil joined me.

"You still think it's a coincidence?" I said, kneeling to examine the tracks, which appeared to have been made in the night, since nothing had eroded them except for the rain.

Cecil took off his hat to scratch his bald head then put it back on again. "I don't know what to think, Garth. Somebody's been here, that's for sure."

"Do you know who owns this property?"

"No. But I can find out."

"It might be a place to start."

Then I noticed a set of footprints leading away from where the car had been parked. We followed them to the edge of the lake and back again. A whole lot smaller than mine, they looked like a woman's footprints to me.

"What do you think, Cecil?" I asked about the footprints.

"Neither one of us could fit in those shoes."

"Do you think they were made by a woman?"

"That or a kid."

"Most kids don't drive cars. Or pickups, if that turns out to be the case."

"That's about all they do drive around here, Garth."

"I'm talking about a kid small enough to fit those tracks."

"It could still be a small boy. I'm not ruling that out."

"I'm not asking you to."

We climbed back into the Impala and continued on around the lake. None of the permanent residents that we talked to knew who owned the property in question, or remembered seeing anything out of the ordinary the night before. We were about to give up, when we came to a home on the hill directly across the lake from where the fire had been. There, an elderly man wearing jeans, a patched red-and-black plaid wool shirt, and scuffed brown Wolverine hiking boots swore he saw lights across the lake right before he went to bed.

"What time was that?" Cecil said.

"Midnight, or thereabouts. Mother was already in bed. I'd fallen asleep watching the news and went into the kitchen to put my coffee cup in the sink."

"Mother" in this case was his wife, a stout, gray-haired, cheerful woman now in the kitchen baking bread. The kitchen led through a sliding door out onto a large cedar deck that overlooked a half acre of yard and a good chunk of Coon Lake. We stood in the living room. Its floor and walls were varnished to a high gloss, a fire burned in its native stone fireplace, and the faint smoky scent of pine, along with that of freshly baked bread was in the air.

"Does it happen often that you see lights across the way?" I said.

"Not this time of year. That's why I took note of it. Of course, in summer the kids fairly wear out these roads going from one party to the next."

"Do you remember the fire a couple years ago?" I said.

The man's face said that he did. "That's not something that you're likely to forget. Especially if you're the one who called it in. What brought that up anyway?"

"Fickle Store burned last night. There are similarities between the fire last night and the one across the lake, though I'd rather not say what they are."

"You hear that, Mother?" The man wore a look of shocked concern. "Fickle Store burned last night."

"I heard."

"Now where are we to go when we run out of something? That new store up the road is not scheduled to be built until next summer."

"What store is that?" I said.

"It's one of those convenience stores that sell everything from gas to groceries to lottery tickets. Sort of like Fickle Store, but with a lot more choices. There's one supposed to go in there where County Road J crosses Coon Lake Road, along with a marina and a restaurant."

"That's less than a mile away," Cecil said.

The man rubbed his hands together from either worry or anticipation. "Don't we know it."

We thanked him and were about to leave when I said, "You happen to know who owns that property across the lake?"

He thought a moment, but couldn't come up with anything.

"Bolin," Mother said from the kitchen.

"That's right. A man by the name of Bolin over in White Lick owns it. Why, you looking to buy it? If so, I hear he's looking to sell it cheap."

"Why's that?"

"He claims the place is haunted. You know of course that's where the man and his daughter that drowned lived. What was that, Mother, 25, 30 years ago?"

"Something like that."

"Then there was supposed to have been a suicide several years before the drowning, but I don't recall that happening. We didn't move here until 1965."

"Sixty-four," was the word from the kitchen.

"Sixty-four. The thing is, Bolin's been trying to unload that property for the past two years with no takers. He's definitely in the mood to deal."

"Good luck," I heard Cecil say under his breath.

"You have time to go over to White Lick with me?" Cecil asked, as we stopped at the intersection of County Road

J and Coon Lake Road, the site of the future marina and convenience store.

"No. I'm already behind as it is."

"Then what should I ask when I get there?"

"As little as possible. Let him do the talking."

Cecil turned right onto County Road J and headed toward Oakalla. "I don't like this, Garth. As you're fond of saying, it looks like it has roots."

"It's starting to," I admitted.

"What's your take so far?"

"I'll reserve judgment until you get back from White Lick."

"What about the pickup? You going to follow up on it?"

"As soon as we get home."

CHAPTER 6

Cecil let me off at the Marathon, then made a U-turn and drove back down Perrin Street to Fickle Road on his way to White Lick. The rain, which fell straight down with the monotony of clockwork, appeared to have set in for the day. The streets of Oakalla, rain-slickened and empty, looked like the mean streets of a Charles Dickens novel.

"The pickup out back?" I asked Danny, who was changing the oil in a Ford Taurus.

"What pickup is that?"

"The one that was in Beezer's alfalfa field."

"Damn. I knew there was something I was forgetting."

"You're not putting me on?"

Danny opened five quarts of 10-W-30 Valvoline and poured them one at a time into a blue funnel that he'd stuck into the block of the Taurus. "No, I'm not putting you on. What with the fire and all, I've been behind all morning. But I'll get to it as soon as Sniffy gets back from lunch."

"Don't bother. It's not there," I said.

"Then where is it?"

"I don't know. But Beezer said this morning at breakfast that it was gone."

"Good riddance?" Danny offered.

"I want to think so. But someone driving that same truck, or its twin brother, stole ten dollars worth of gas off of Jasper Peterson night before last. Jasper claims a similar thing happened when that cabin burned over on Coon Lake a couple years ago. Cecil and I drove over there and found where someone had recently parked in the snow where the cabin used to be."

Danny checked the dip stick to make sure the Taurus was filled to the right level, wiped his hands, and joined me at his desk, where he began to figure the bill.

"I'm sorry to hear you say that," he said. "I found a burned out two-gallon gas can in both that cabin, and the basement of Fickle Store. I thought it was a coincidence until now."

"It still might be."

"One can only hope."

"Was there any sign of forced entry last night?" I said.

"No. The place was locked up tight when we got there. Jasper swears he was awake at the time and didn't hear anyone breaking in."

"So how did he or she get in?"

"She?" Danny was quick to note.

"Humor me."

"There's a coal chute on the east side of the basement from years ago. My guess is that they could have gone in there, then out any of the doors."

"But how would they know about the coal chute?" I said.

"Maybe they'd slid down it before."

"That doesn't seem likely." I headed for the door.

"Why not?" Danny said.

"Coal went out around here sometime in the 50s."

"But the chute didn't. It's still there. And if you're looking for a way in, you'll find one."

"I guess."

He glanced down at the bill for the Taurus, saw nothing written there, and started his figuring all over again. "Where to now?" he said.

"Lunch, then my office."

"If I happen to run across that pickup, do you want to know about it?"

"Yes."

Danny looked up at me. "What's going on, Garth? You have any idea?"

"Not a clue."

"Comforting."

"Isn't it though."

———————

It was quiet inside the Corner Bar and Grill. One look around the lunchroom told me why. A stranger sat in our midst there on the red-vinyl-covered stool where I usually sat to eat my lunch. He looked a little too surly and a whole lot too large for me to ask him to move, so I took a seat to his immediate right. Except for either end of the counter and the stool where he sat, I had my choice of seats.

The stranger gave me a quick, sharp glance as if I'd invaded his space, but said nothing to me. He had short brown hair, a two-day growth of beard, a bulky, tough-guy build and demeanor, and was wearing designer jeans and a brown leather jacket. A spoiled rich man's son was my first impression of him.

"I hear you've been looking for a pickup. You find it yet?" I said.

"Sir?" He turned to look at me. Amend that to a spoiled rich man's son with the cool sleepy eyes of a gator.

"I heard you were looking for a black pickup with a Confederate flag on the front. I just wondered if you found it."

"Who wants to know?"

I took my special deputy's badge out of my wallet and laid it on the counter in front of him. "It's for real. You can ask anyone in here."

His broad boyish smile was so spontaneous and unaffected, it took me off guard. I was expecting any reaction but that.

"If I could ever get y'all to talk to me," he said in a soft southern drawl. "I swear I haven't been this deep in frost since my ex-wife left home."

He offered me his hand and I shook it. His was the

loose, too relaxed grip of a man who knows his own strength and fears it.

"Larry Don Loomus," he said.

"Garth Ryland."

"Is there someplace private we could talk?"

"Follow me."

We went into the barroom, which was deserted, and sat at the back booth where Abby and I had sat during our first date. Two years wasn't all that long ago, but with everything that had happened in the interim, it seemed an eternity.

"Larry Don Loomus," I said. "The name is familiar."

"I used to play some football a while back." For some reason that memory was a painful one.

"LSU?"

"Southern Mississippi."

"Linebacker?" He was about six-two and weighed at least 220. And Sniffy was right when he said that none of it was fat.

"Running-back."

Now, I remembered. His senior year in college he was the nation's leading rusher and being lauded as a Heisman Trophy candidate when he got injured and just dropped out of sight, like a rock down a well.

"What happened? Was it your knee?"

He shook his head no. "You remember on Monday Night Football when Lawrence Taylor made a pretzel out of Joe Theismann's leg? That's what happened to me in our game with Old Miss."

What he meant was that he had suffered a compound fracture as Joe Theismann had, which is when the bone splinters and comes out through the skin. Joe Theismann's injury had ended his career as quarterback for the Washington Redskins.

He went on to say, "When they set it, it didn't take the way it should have and didn't heal right. It doesn't bother me so much at home, but up here in the cold, it's pure misery."

"Wait until it really gets cold," I said.

"I don't plan on being here that long." Though he smiled, there was an effort behind it.

"Did you play with Bret Favre?" I said, remembering that he also had played for the University of Southern Mississippi.

"In his shadow."

"You ever think that could have been you?"

"Every single day of my life."

I let the topic lie. It was obvious that Larry Don Loomus once had big dreams for himself, and it was equally obvious that they had come crashing down around him.

"So what are you doing in Oakalla, Wisconsin?"

He took out his wallet and showed me his private investigator's license, which had been issued by the state of Louisiana. "I'm looking for someone," he said.

"Anyone I might know?"

"That depends." He flipped through his wallet until he found the photograph for which he was looking. "You see anyone that looks like her around here lately?"

I examined the photograph and said no. The woman in the photograph appeared to be about 25 and had long straight jet-black hair, bright almond eyes, and the dark narrow oval face of an Egyptian princess. She was beautiful. Any man who still had a pulse would stop to take a second look at her.

"She's familiar, though."

He gave me a curious look. It was somewhere between interest and disbelief, as if he'd just drawn to an inside straight. "What do you mean?"

"I mean that I think I've seen her before, but not lately. Is she from around here?"

"No. But she's supposed to have family in the area."

"Do you have their name?"

"No. I wasn't given it."

"Do you have her name?"

"Camelia Capers."

"No Capers around here that I know of."

"So I've been told."

We were interrupted, as Bernice brought Larry Don Loomus his lunch—a double cheeseburger with fries and a bottle of Bud Light. Then she took my order.

"French fry?" he said, offering me his plate.

"Don't mind if I do."

I had the special of the day, which was bratwurst and German potato salad. I passed up Larry Don's offer of a beer and instead drank water with my meal. If I drank a beer at noon on a dreary day like this, I'd soon be curled up on my desk, asleep for the duration.

"You've been asking all the questions," he said when he finished his cheeseburger and I finished his last remaining french fry. "Y'all mind if I ask a couple?"

"Fire away."

"This pickup that we're both looking for. What's your interest in it?"

Despite his easy-going style and soft southern drawl that would charm a possum out of a persimmon tree, Larry Don's eyes still looked gator ready to me. Right at the center of their deep placid pools, I could see two caldrons.

"The pickup was rumored to be at the scene of a fire a few hours before it started. Is Camelia Capers capable of arson?"

"I wouldn't know."

I couldn't tell if he were lying. His eyes never seemed to change much, even to blink.

"What *do* you know about her?" I said.

"I know that she's been missing for a week from Emerald City and that I was hired to find her. That's all."

"Where's Emerald City? Louisiana?"

"Mississippi. Way down south, due west of Sandy Hook."

"Is it on the map?"

"No. It's the name of a place. Not a town."

"What sort of place?"

"A religious place," he seemed uncomfortable saying.

"You mean it's a cult?"

"I said I don't know." He was trying to be polite, but

it wasn't easy. He'd much rather ask the questions than answer them.

"Well, if it isn't a cult and she hasn't broken any laws, why would they care where Camelia Capers is and why would they hire a private detective from Louisiana to find her? You are from Louisiana, aren't you?"

"Sir? I don't understand your question. Or maybe it's better that I don't understand it."

"My question is, why would Emerald City, whatever it is, go all the way to New Orleans to hire a private detective?"

"Because I have the reputation of always getting my man."

"And woman?"

He smiled. It was meant to be disarming, but came off as arrogant. "That goes without saying."

"Then you're good at what you do?"

"I am the *best* at what I do. Make no mistake about that."

"And humble, too."

"As my daddy used to say, humility is a smiling cur dog that'll bite you as soon as your back is turned."

"I'll try to remember that."

"That would be my advice."

"Which leads us back to Emerald City. Why would a religious place that's not a cult want someone back badly enough to hire, by his own admission, the world's greatest private detective?"

"Are you poking fun at me, Mr. Ryland? If so, I don't

see the humor." Lucky for me, I was on my own turf, or he might have *me* for lunch.

"No, I'm trying to find out what's going on," I said. "And so far I haven't."

Larry Don appraised me coolly, then for whatever his reason said, "It's my understanding that Camelia Capers left Emerald City with a sizable amount of money that was not her own."

"How much money?"

"That I don't have to tell you. Sir." He rose, preparing to leave.

"Aren't you forgetting something?" I said.

His eyes searched the table then gave me a questioning look.

"The pickup. You didn't ask if I'd found it."

"Have you?" He would be surprised if I had.

"No. But I know where it's been, where it was the last time anyone saw it."

"That much I've managed to learn myself. Good day, Mr. Ryland. I'm sure we'll meet again."

I watched him limp through the swinging barroom door, which closed with a swoosh behind him. Then I left lunch money and tip beside my plate and went out the north door of the barroom into the rain.

CHAPTER 7

Once at my office, I made a call to the Wisconsin State Police post at Madison and asked for Trooper Michael Higgins. He was out on patrol, but barring an emergency was expected in by four. I told the dispatcher to have him call me then.

I spent the rest of the afternoon calling advertisers and laying out that week's paper, which would go to press late Thursday night or early Friday morning. As yet, I didn't have an idea for my column, but would worry about that come Thursday. Ever since I'd stepped down off my soapbox at Ruth's request, I'd found my weekly columns harder and harder to write. So either I needed to spend more time digging for some new material or get back on my soapbox again. Not a researcher at heart, and at the risk of displeasing Ruth, I decided that I probably would take the easy way out.

The rain continued to fall throughout the afternoon

until it had completely washed away the last traces of Sunday night's snow. Also washed away were any hopes I might have of matching the pickup's tires to those tracks left at Coon Lake. It was a long shot to begin with, and now that the pickup was missing, an even longer one, but it would have been nice to know if the pickup could be linked to the fire at Fickle Store, or if its being there at the store Sunday night was only a coincidence.

The phone rang. Thirty seconds later, and I'd have been out the door and on my way home.

"Michael Higgins here," the fresh, bold, unmistakably Wisconsin voice said. "I've got a note that says I'm supposed to call you."

"I just wanted to thank you for turning that pickup over to me."

"What pickup are you talking about?" he said in mock innocence.

"The one I'm now looking for in connection with the arson fire at Fickle Store."

"That's news to me. The arson part."

"I guess we can wait until the state fire marshal makes it official."

What do you need to know?"

"We've got a man here named Larry Don Loomus, who says he's a private eye from New Orleans, who's looking for a Camelia Capers, who supposedly stole a large sum of money from a 'religious place' in southern Mississippi named Emerald City. I'd like for you to check all three of them out for me—Larry Don Loomus, Camelia Capers, and Emerald City."

"I assume you have your reasons."

"Camelia Capers, who supposedly has relatives in this area, is also the one supposedly driving the pickup that drove off with ten dollars worth of stolen gas from Fickle Store Sunday evening. When Marshal Hardwick and I examined that same pickup yesterday morning, we found two large caliber slugs in it and what appeared to be blood on the seat."

"Did you impound it?"

"No. The wrecker at the Marathon was down and by the time it was fixed, the pickup was gone."

"So now you're hoping for damage control."

"No. That's a term you cops like to use. I'm trying to get to the bottom of this mess before somebody else gets hurt."

"Somebody else?"

"I'm thinking of Camelia Capers, or perhaps a companion. That blood had to come from someone."

"I'll see what I can do."

"I'll appreciate it."

I closed up shop for the time being and started walking home in the rain when I met Cecil in his patrol car driving east along Gas Line Road. He stopped the car and motioned for me to get inside.

"Need a ride home?" he said. With half moons the size of small craters under his bloodshot eyes, Cecil looked like I felt—one nod away from a long winter's nap.

"If you're offering. What did you learn in White Lick?"

Cecil proceeded on to Berry Street and turned left. "That Carl Bolin is a hard man to get hold of. He has irons in a lot of fires and doesn't like to stay too long in one place."

"What sort of fires?"

"Poor choice of words. Real estate, development, antiques, that sort of thing. It was interesting to learn that he also owns the land where that new convenience store and marina are supposed to go in there at the crossroads."

"Food for thought," I said, "in light of the fact that his only would be competitor for miles around just had a fire."

"Here's some more food for thought." We stopped at the junction of Berry Street and Jackson Street and waited for a couple cars to pass. "Carl Bolin hasn't owned that property where the cabin burned for very long. He only bought it after the fire, thinking that he could turn a quick buck on it." We turned west on Jackson Street.

"Why were the owners willing to sell?"

"Like that man across the lake said yesterday, they claimed it was haunted—by the girl who drowned in the lake."

"They ever see her?" As in all such matters, I was a skeptic, even though I could claim a couple ghosts of my own.

"They said they did. Summer nights, after everyone was off the lake, they'd see her walking the shore."

"As long as they didn't see her walking on the water."

"I'm serious, Garth. Carl Bolin says the same thing, which is why he's so willing to cut his losses and move on."

We stopped at the four-way stop uptown then made a right onto Home Street. Like a lot of streets in Oakalla that changed their names once they crossed Jackson, Home Street became School Street south of Jackson and remained that all the way to the grain elevator. There it came to a dead end at the railroad tracks that ran behind the elevator.

"What does the ghost look like?" I said.

"A young woman with long dark hair is what they said."

"Dressed all in white?"

Cecil saw where I was headed, but still couldn't avoid the trap. "Yes. Dressed all in white."

When we stopped in front of my house, I was delighted to see a light on inside. I rolled down my window to see if I could smell supper cooking and was rewarded with the smell of meat browning.

I said, "You find out the name of the people who owned the cabin when it burned?"

"A family by the name of Friedhofer. But it's my understanding they're no longer in the area."

"It might help to talk to them," I said.

"I'll see what I can do."

"You did good work today, Cecil."

"For the good it did," he said wearily.

"You never know." Since he seemed not to hear, I said, "Was there something else?"

"It might matter. It might not. Carl Bolin is Ulma Friedrickson's son by a previous marriage."

"The same Ulma Friedrickson who sold Fickle Store to Jasper Peterson?"

"Yes."

"What did Carl Bolin think about the sale?"

"He didn't take it well from what I understand. Then there's one other thing, Garth. Jasper said that he was nicked for ten dollars worth of gas. Danny said he found a two-gallon can in the basement of Fickle Store. That leaves a couple of gallons of gas still unaccounted for."

"Maybe all or some of it went in the truck."

"And maybe it didn't."

I went inside where Ruth was browning cuts of round steak in her Dutch oven in preparation for baking it. This was one of those chill damp nights when a fire in the fireplace would have gone well with a good book and a glass of brandy. You'd read until your lids were too heavy to lift anymore, then drift peacefully off to sleep in your favorite chair, letting the rest of the world take a hike. One of those nights I'd forgo, had forgone too many times to count, on which I would look back with a sigh.

"You look like you could use some sleep," Ruth said, as I took a seat at the kitchen table.

I glanced at the round red clock with the yellow face and black numerals that hung on the wall above the sink. Five-thirty p.m., and already it was pitch dark out.

"I *could* use some sleep. Getting up and going to a fire in the middle of the night will do that to you."

"Getting up and going to the shelter will do the same thing. At least you got the chance to go back to bed."

"For the good it did."

Daisy, who had been sitting by the back door wanting out, came over to put her head in my lap, then sighed in contentment as I scratched behind her ears. Daisy was Abby's lemon-spotted English setter, who was staying with Ruth and me while Abby was in Detroit. An outdoor dog at heart, she saw no reason not to be out in the rain.

"Why don't I let her out?" I said. "The worst she'll do is muddy up the basement."

"And everything in between."

Ruth had a point. But I let Daisy out anyway.

"By the way, how's your charge?" I sat down again at the kitchen table.

"What charge?"

Ruth was peeling potatoes that would soon go in with the baked steak. And if she held true to form, we'd also have some of the sweet corn that she'd canned summer before last.

"The one at the shelter. The one that you went out into the night to admit."

"She's doing fine," Ruth said.

"Anyone I know?"

She didn't answer, which meant that it probably was.

"I had an interesting day. Would you like to hear about it?" I said.

"I'm listening."

I told her about my encounter with Larry Don

Loomus, Cecil's and my trip to Fickle and Coon Lake, and the ghost with long dark hair.

"So Cecil thinks Jasper Peterson burned down his own store for the insurance money," Ruth said.

"That's what he thinks. Why?"

"Because it's not the first time that Fickle Store has burned down. It burned down right after Jasper bought it."

"He never told me that when I interviewed him a couple years ago, and he didn't mention it today."

"I don't think it's something he wants to advertise."

"Why? Was that fire thought to be arson?"

"That was the general feeling around here. But it was never proven."

"Was Jasper under any suspicion?"

"You're always under suspicion, Garth, whenever something you own burns down."

"So Jasper came out of the fire okay?"

"As things turned out, yes."

"What about the fire over on Coon Lake two years ago? You have any thoughts about that?"

Ruth threw the peelings into the waste basket then began to slice the potatoes lengthwise. There was enough there to feed four lumberjacks, but since she claimed to have survived the Great Depression on turnips and peanut butter sandwiches, Ruth never shorted us on any meal.

"No," she said in answer to my question. "But the man who drowned was once the pastor here at the Methodist Church. His name was Israel Hammond."

"What about his daughter, the one who drowned with him? Do you remember her?"

"I really don't recall much about him or his family. Karl and I were going to Fair Haven then. Except his wife was sort of quiet and sour and his daughter, if I'm thinking right, was as pretty as a picture. They weren't here for very long, a year or two at most."

"What about her hair? Do you remember whether she wore it long or short, or what color it was?"

"Long, I think. And it was dark."

I studied her to see if she was serious. "You're putting me on, aren't you?"

"Ask a foolish question. My memory's good, but it's not that good, Garth. There might even have been other children besides the one daughter."

"Was Israel Hammond living in Oakalla when he died?"

"No. He'd moved on by then."

"His wife still around?"

"You need to ask Beulah Peters about that. It's my understanding she and Mrs. Hammond have stayed in touch."

"How do you know that?"

"I read it in your paper. Maybe you should read what you write sometime."

"You can't expect me to remember every little detail like you do."

"Why not, since you're the one who always needs to know."

Since this was an argument I couldn't win, I changed the subject. "Camelia Capers. What do you think about her?"

"I don't have any thoughts about her. I'm not sure you should have either. You don't even know she exists. All you have is a stranger's word on that."

I got up to let Daisy in before she wore a hole in the storm door. "You forgot to wipe your feet," I said, as she tracked mud from the utility room all the way to the kitchen.

Once, when I first knew her, Ruth would have banished both Daisy and me to the basement without our supper. Now, she merely sighed, tore off a wad of paper towels, and handed it to me. Daisy, to show her appreciation, followed me around the floor, licking my ear every time I bent over.

"Camelia Capers exists, Ruth. I saw a photograph of her. And she's strangely familiar, though I don't know why."

"What does she look like?"

"Long black hair, almond eyes, a long dark oval face that you might see on a super model. It's my guess that she has some Creole blood in her."

Ruth had stopped her work and stood at the counter listening. For the first time that evening I had her full attention.

"How could she be familiar? We don't have any Capers in town," Ruth said.

"It could be her married name."

"Is she married?"

"I don't know. I'll have to ask Larry Don the next time I see him."

"In the meantime you might try to find that pickup. It sounds like it has its own story to tell."

"If I knew where to look."

She mumbled something to herself that I couldn't understand.

"What's that, Ruth?"

She was at the sink, rinsing potatoes. "The pickup. I said it can't have gone far—or somebody would have seen it."

"Not if it went at night. It could be all the way to Canada by now. Or back down in Mississippi."

"Canada would be my guess," she said.

"Mine, too. Why is it yours?"

"Because, from everything you've told me about that pickup, it sounds like a truck on the run."

"And Camelia Capers, might she not be on the run, too?"

Ruth's look was one of reflection and concern. "That goes without saying."

CHAPTER 8

Much to my relief, the rest of that night and the following morning went quietly. I worked until midnight on the *Oakalla Reporter*, trying to catch up, then rose early the next morning for more of the same. The rain had become a hard gritty snow in the night, but not much else about the weather had changed. The sky, low and gray, had a few more black humps in it, and the wind, gone from east to north-northwest, had a bite to it, but only a cock-eyed optimist would call that an improvement.. The cause of the whole mess was a cut off low pressure hovering over Lake Superior, taking its own sweet time about moving on. Meanwhile, we'd just have to grin and bear it. Or bitch, as I preferred to do.

At noon I walked to the Corner Bar and Grill for lunch, ordered a cheeseburger with fried onions, macaroni salad, and iced tea, and sat there pleased to be eating my lunch in peace, when Bernice approached me with a worried look on her face.

"Whatever it is, I don't want to hear it," I said.

"All I was going to ask is if you'd seen Beezer today?"

"No. Why?"

"He missed supper last night and breakfast this morning. Since you two were last seen riding away on his Moped, I thought maybe you knew something I didn't."

"Maybe the weather's keeping him away," I said.

"It never has before. Beezer never misses a meal here. You and I both know that."

"He misses lunch."

"He doesn't eat what we'd call lunch. Here, home, anywhere else. The way he tells it, he doesn't even keep any food in the house except to snack on."

"You might mention your concern to Marshal Hardwick the next time you see him," I said, afraid of where we were headed.

"If I see him. He doesn't get in here nearly as often as you do. Neither does anyone else lately. Even Hiram mentioned how dead it was in here last night."

I looked around the lunchroom and counted only two other people besides myself. "It's the weather, Bernice. People don't like to go out in it. Once we get resigned to it, you'll see the difference."

"Easy to say if your livelihood doesn't depend on it."

"Bernice, you have the only restaurant and bar in town, and this is Wisconsin, for God's sake. Most towns have more bars than churches, and we've got three of those, four counting Fair Haven. So don't expect a whole lot of sympathy from me."

"And how many newspapers are there in town?" she shot back. "And how many times have I heard you crying in your beer over just one lost subscriber?"

I eyed my cheeseburger, wanting to eat it before it got stone cold. "Okay. As soon as I finish lunch, I'll go check on Beezer."

"Thank you," she said with a smile that made me think I'd just been snookered.

The only thing in my favor on the long walk out to Beezer's was that the wind was at my back. With the air temperature right at freezing, most of the snow that fell melted as soon as it hit the ground and that which didn't melt, stuck either in the tall grass alongside Gas Line Road, or on the cornstalks in Gene Siegfried's field, or on the brush piled along the old interurban right of way, or on the windrows of fallen leaves, whose glazed brown humps made me think of gingerbread and powder sugar donuts.

Beezer's Moped, with a dusting of snow on its seat, leaned against the old iron pump in front of his cabin. His jack pines and cedars were likewise dusted with snow, as were the stack of firewood on his front porch and the rusted iron wagon wheel buried up to mid-spoke in duff.

"Beezer?" I shouted, after knocking twice on the cabin door without an answer.

I tripped the latch and went inside to discover that Beezer wasn't there, and hadn't been there for some time. His wood stove had a remnant of warmth, but no live coals. The cabin, too, had a remnant of warmth, but the longer I stood, the cooler I grew until I had to move to ward off the chill seeping into me.

Beezer had chinked the walls since I had last been in there and replaced the cracked panes in the cabin's two windows. But there were still no rugs on the floor, and except for the empty pair of deer legs that Beezer used as a gun rack, no furnishings on the wall, and no creature comforts of any kind. What there was were the worn pine floor, the dark pine walls, a small wooden table and a wooden chair at each end of it, a dark-red vinyl up-holstered couch with brass studs, a long white slit in its backrest and a brass lamp hanging over the coverless blue-and-white striped feather pillow scrunched up against the armrest, a daybed piled high with quilts parked under the east window, and a floor-to-ceiling bookcase filled with books.

Books by Sigurd Olson, Aldo Leopold, John Muir, and Ernest Thompson Seton; Zane Gray, Jack London, Horatio Alger, and Harold Bell Wright. Novels, nature books, and biographies, an 1850 McGuffey's reader, and an 1887 *Adams County History*; all were in respectable shape and most of them were older than I was. They made me hope that Beezer's absence was only tempo-rary. Otherwise, I would have to steal them to save them from ruin.

I went out Beezer's south door to his ramshackle barn with the rusted tin roof where his Buick Roadmaster was parked. The Roadmaster still carried the V-dent in its grill from its collision with Delpha Wright's willow tree and bits of wood from the tree itself. The fact that it was still there told me that Beezer hadn't taken it wherever he had gone. With a sigh of resignation, I dragged open the wooden gate behind the barn and started for the woods.

Soon among the pines, I followed a small, step-across stream to its junction with another small stream and then the merged stream into a small meadow surrounded on each side by hills of scrub oak. All had been quiet within the pines, their thick green fur a barrier to wind and snow alike, but once out in the open meadow I could hear the wind rattle the dead oak leaves clinging to the trees, and the snow as it salted the rushes and cattails along the stream.

Every few steps I would stop to look and listen. Beezer's gun rack was empty, so perhaps he had gone hunting and had an accident of some kind, or had suffered a heart attack, and was either dead or so badly hurt that he couldn't make it out on his own. That was the best-case scenario, which made me alert for any sight or sound that might tell me where he was. The worse-case scenario was that he had blundered into something sinister, and gotten himself killed.

Where the meadow narrowed at its neck and the hills of scrub oaks closed in around it, I came to a large double-sided corncrib that was remarkably well preserved, considering its age. Like Beezer's barn, the corncrib had a high stone foundation, a tin roof, and had weathered over the years to a tattletale gray. Unlike the barn, the corncrib had no side boards missing, or holes in its roof, or sway in its ridge rafter. All of which should have given me fair warning before I looked inside.

The purple-black pickup, one-eyed, still decked in red mud, was enough of a shock, but sitting on its hood, staring out at me through amber-glass eyes was the largest deer head and rack I had ever seen. Old Elmo? It had to be.

I searched the pickup, being careful not to disturb Old Elmo's perch there, but found nothing I hadn't seen before. The bed of the pickup was empty, as was the corn crib, except for what you might expect to find there—corn cobs and rat holes. Beezer was nowhere in sight. Neither was the body of Old Elmo. I was then left with the inevitable question: Who had killed Old Elmo and why? To that I had to add the original question: Where had Beezer gone, and why?

The stream made a left turn before it reached the corncrib, so whoever had driven the pickup the length of Beezer's alfalfa field and then down the hill to the corn-crib didn't have to jump the creek. But they did have to drive over a few small scrub oaks on their way down the hill, so it wasn't hard to find the way they'd come.

At the top of the hill I debated on whether to continue my search for Beezer and decided against it. In the first place, I doubted that I would find him. In the second place, I didn't like the feeling that had been lodged in my gut ever since I'd found Old Elmo's head on top of the pickup. I couldn't be sure that someone was watching my every move, but I couldn't be sure he wasn't either. "Discretion is the better part of valor," my father was fond of saying. I chose to listen to him for once and got out of there.

My phone rang the moment I entered my office. "Ryland here," I said.

"Michael Higgins here. You sound out of sorts. Is something wrong?"

"You don't want to know. What do you have for me, Michael?"

"On the plus side, Larry Don Loomus appears to be legitimate. I called his office in New Orleans and his secretary said that he was out of town on a case. Did you know, by the way, that he made honorable mention All-American his senior year at Southern Mississippi? That he would likely have made first team if he hadn't been injured?"

"Yes, I know. What about Camelia Capers?"

"Did I catch you at a bad time, Garth? You still don't sound right to me."

I hung my head and counted to ten.

"Garth?"

"I'm here, Michael. But now I've got a missing person

on my hands along with everything else that's going on. And Old Elmo's head on the hood of a pickup, but don't ask me to explain that. So yes, I'm not only out of sorts, but out of breath after wading through a goddamn alfalfa field that must be at least ten miles long. But that's my problem, not yours. So I'm sorry."

"Who's missing?" he said, the cop in him curious.

"Beezer Portnoy. He's the one who owns the field where the pickup was parked."

"For how long?"

"Since sometime yesterday. He and I ate breakfast together at the Corner Bar and Grill, but that's the last anyone has seen of him. I know he went directly home from there, but he's not at home, even though his Moped is."

"You want help looking for him?"

"Not at the moment. I found the pickup, hidden in a corncrib back in Beezer's woods. Whoever put it there did so for a reason, either to hide it from someone else, or to keep it out of sight until he or she needed it again. We have too much traffic in and out of there, we're going to scare them away."

"What about Beezer Portnoy?"

"Beezer is a woodsman, has been all of his life. If he's alive, and I have no reason except for his absence to believe that he isn't, then wherever he is, he can take care of himself. If he's dead, we can't help him any—except to catch his killer."

"By staking out the pickup?"

"Yes. I'll check on it from time to time."

"Then what do you want from me?"

I ignored him for a moment, thinking that someone was tapping on my north window. It turned out to be the snow.

"I want you to find out who burned down Fickle Store."

"As you predicted, so does the state fire marshal. But we have an arson team for that."

"Why haven't I seen them around?"

"Priorities." Meaning that when it came to arson fires, a country grocery store sucked hind tit.

"Then tell me what you know about Camelia Capers," I said.

"Hers is not a fairy tale."

"Somehow I'm not surprised."

"Camelia Capers is from Hattiesburg, Mississippi. She graduated from a private girls' school there and attended the University of Southern Mississippi until her sophomore year when she was put on probation for possession of marijuana and subsequently dropped out of school. Two years later she was arrested for prostitution in Jackson, then the year after that, and the year after that, each time receiving a fine and probation. Subsequently, she was admitted to Hinds General Hospital following a drug overdose then released into the care of Orion, Emerald City, Mississippi."

"Who the hell is Orion?"

"I'm getting to that. Camelia Capers is 29 years old. She's 5-10, weighs 130, with black hair, brown eyes, and a beauty mark on her right cheek. Her last known address is Emerald City, Mississippi." He cleared his throat then said, "Any questions about Orion and Emerald City need to be referred to Stonewall Jackson Huff, sheriff of Isabella County, Mississippi. He said, and I'm quoting him now, that he would consider it a favor if you did not call him until after six, as five to six is his supper hour."

"That Central Standard Time?" I said.

"I think so."

"You have his number?"

He gave it to me.

"Be a damn shame to interrupt his supper hour," I said.

"Get some sleep, Garth. You sound like you need it."

"Thanks, Michael. First chance I get."

I hung up and sat back in my chair. There was no use trying to get any work done because Cecil's brown Impala was already slowing down as it passed by on Gas Line Road.

Cecil came into my office without knocking, stamping the snow off his boots as he did. Though there was no prediction of a heavy snow, it seemed to be coming down in a hurry, an observation that wasn't lost on Cecil, who cast a worried glance outside.

"Where's all this coming from?" he said.

"You're talking to the wrong guy. What did you find out about the Friedhofer family?"

"They're living in Naples, Florida. They say they like their winters a whole lot better now."

Cecil took a seat in one of the two rock-hard chairs that I kept jammed up against the east wall to discourage visitors. I had enough interruptions as it was without trying to make everyone who entered my office feel welcome.

"Did they confirm Carl Bolin's ghost story?"

Cecil put his hat in his lap, clasped his hands behind his head, and leaned back against the wall. The ease with which he did that reminded me of Rupert Roberts. Maybe, if we could survive the present, there was hope for Cecil and me after all.

He said, "They not only confirmed what Carl Bolin said, but added to the list. They swore they saw her at least a half dozen times."

"Always walking the shoreline?"

"Yes. They said she seemed to like summer nights best. Once, they claim, they saw her go into the water and didn't see her come out again."

"When was the last time they saw her?"

"They didn't say."

"Pardon my skepticism, Cecil, but how did they know that she was a ghost and not one of their neighbors out for a midnight stroll?"

"By what she wore. You asked yesterday if she was dressed all in white. Well, I asked them about that to make sure. She was. In an angel robe, the way they describe it."

"Carrying a harp, no doubt."

"What's that, Garth?"

"Never mind, Cecil. People see what they want to see and there's no use arguing otherwise."

"They say their next door neighbors saw her, too. They tried to take a picture of her, but it didn't turn out."

"It never does."

Cecil rose with a sigh and put his hat back on. "I'm only telling you what they told me, Garth. I didn't say I believed them."

"I believe them. But I doubt it was a ghost they saw."

"What then?"

"I don't know. I do think, though, that we've taken that angle about as far as we can go for now. Maybe we ought to look somewhere else closer to home for answers."

"Say the word."

"The first thing you can do is to talk to Hattie Peeler and ask her if she saw the pickup being moved night before last. I'm curious as to whether it could have been used in the fire at Fickle Store. And Beezer is missing. After you talk to Hattie, drive on out to his place on the odd chance that he's back home again."

"How long has Beezer been missing?"

"Since yesterday morning."

"Maybe he took the pickup somewhere."

"I don't think so, Cecil. The pickup was already gone before Beezer disappeared. And . . ." I started to tell him about finding the pickup then changed my mind. As I told Michael Higgins, I didn't want any more traffic out there than absolutely necessary, and with what I knew about Cecil, he might feel the need to stake it out. And like Beezer, end up missing.

"And what?"

"Tell Hattie to let you or me know the minute that pickup shows up again."

"Do you honestly think it will?"

"Yes, Cecil, I do."

He studied me for a moment before saying, "What aren't you telling me, Garth?"

"County business," was all I said.

"I thought we had the start of a team," he said, his feelings hurt.

"We do. And don't leave thinking that Rupert Roberts and I never kept anything from each other. We did. Or that Ruth and I don't still."

"Why? That's all I want to know."

He deserved the truth, but I wasn't sure that I could give it to him without hurting his feelings further. A white lie? A black lie? Who really knew which was which? Both were deceitful and self-serving. So you called them as you saw them and learned to live with it.

"Because you don't carry a gun, Cecil."

"So I'm not a real cop?"

"No. Not when it comes right down to it."

"Then why waste your time on me?"

"Because I like you. Because as you just said, we've got a team started. But I don't want you to end up dead because of me. And don't say it can't happen because it nearly did. So if you'll tell me you won't act on what I tell you, I'll tell you what you want to know."

"Nope. I can't promise that."

"I didn't think so."

Thinking we'd said our piece, I turned my attention

to the *Oakalla Reporter*. But when I looked up again, he was still standing there.

"Any other suggestions?" he said.

"About what?"

"Where I might go from here. It'll take me five minutes to talk to Hattie and maybe five more minutes to check up on Beezer."

"I'd revisit both Jasper Peterson and Carl Bolin. Ruth said that Jasper had a convenient fire shortly after he first bought Fickle Store. She also said that Carl Bolin is the son of Ulma Friedrickson, who is the one who sold Jasper the store. See if there's any bad blood between Jasper and Carl Bolin. If there is, see where it leads."

"What will you be doing in the meantime?"

"Trying to put out this week's paper. If I can ever get started."

He took the hint and left. About a half hour later I saw him drive slowly by on his way uptown. Since he didn't stop to tell me what he'd learned from Hattie, or learned at Beezer's, I assumed that (1) his feelings were still hurt, and (2) Beezer was still missing. Not my problem, I decided. Though in my heart of hearts, I knew it was.

Chapter 9

At supper I told Ruth everything about my day except the pickup. I did so partly out of loyalty to Cecil and partly out of suspicion that she wasn't telling me everything she knew about her late-night charge at the shelter. If it came down to a trade, I wanted to have something with which to bargain.

"By the way, Cecil called," she said when I finished. "Not five minutes before you got home."

"What did he have to say?"

"He said that Hattie heard the pickup fire up right after dark and the last she saw of it, it was headed east on Gas Line Road. He went on to say that Beezer wasn't there when he stopped by his cabin."

"East on Gas Line Road?" I said, wondering how it then got where it was.

"That's what Hattie said. I asked him twice to make sure."

"Why twice?"

Ruth put down her knife and fork to glare at me. "Because you don't drive east to get to Canada from here, which is where we agreed the pickup was likely headed."

"Or to get to Fickle Store either," I said, trying that on for size.

Along with pork chops and gravy, we had frozen peas from last year's garden, fried potatoes, and last year's canned peaches for dessert. Our cupboard was growing bare, however. Because of her work at the shelter, Ruth no longer had time to garden and can.

"Why Fickle Store?" she said.

"To burn it down. Why else?"

"For what purpose?"

"I'm working on that. Maybe to set up a diversion."

Bingo. I now had her full attention.

"Go on," she said.

"It would take two or more people, of course. But let's say you wanted to sneak someone somewhere, in or out of the hospital for example, and you didn't want anyone around while you were doing it. What better way than to start a fire that would take everyone, including the town marshal who might be on patrol, out of town?"

"That seems like an awful lot of work," she said, dismissing the idea.

"Not if the stakes were high enough."

"What stakes do you mean?"

Ruth gave her pork chop bone to Daisy, who'd been sitting there lobbying for it for the past five minutes.

Daisy's tactic was tried and true—look as pitiful as possible for as long as possible, but never ever whine or bark.

"The $100,000 or so that Camelia Capers took with her when she left Emerald City. Those are the stakes."

"You don't know she took that much."

"I'm willing to bet."

She ignored me, which likely meant I held the winning hand. "But why go to all the trouble to sneak Camelia Capers into a hospital when you could just as easily sneak her out of town?"

"Because she might be too hurt to travel."

Ruth didn't answer. Instead, she rose and began to clear the table.

"Don't you agree?" I said.

"Agree on what?"

"On what I just said."

"It sounds a little too farfetched to me. In the first place, you can't sneak somebody into a hospital. They have to be admitted."

"My mistake. The shelter, then."

Ruth turned to face me. She wasn't happy with me, but then, that was nothing new.

She said, "Why don't you ask me what you want to know, instead of beating around the bush about it?"

"Fair enough. Did you take Camelia Capers into the shelter late Monday night and is she there now?"

"No comment."

"Guilty as charged."

She reddened with anger. "I'm not guilty of anything,

Garth, except minding my own business, which you might take a lesson from."

"She can't stay there forever. Where's she going to go when she gets out?"

"I don't know and I don't care. I figure that's her problem."

"Then you admit she's there?"

She turned her back to me and began running water for dishes. "As I said, no comment."

"What happens, God forbid, if there's another fire?"

"You can't shame me into anything, Garth. Don't try."

"Then answer me this. Whoever it is that you have at the shelter, how did she get in there?"

"Through the back door."

"Not the front."

"No. She arrived unannounced, Liddy said."

"Suitcase in hand?"

"Empty-handed."

"But injured. Shot, in other words."

Ruth came back to the table for the rest of the supper dishes. "I don't know what's wrong with her, Garth, and that's the truth. She changes her own bandages and looks after herself. All we do is provide her with a bed and three squares a day."

"Does she seem frightened at all?"

"No. She doesn't seem to be afraid of anything or anybody. But I know better."

"How so?"

"Tuesday, when the noon siren went off, she was

already down the stairs and headed for the door before she realized what was going on."

"Do you think it was the siren itself, or the fear of a fire that got to her?"

"I don't know, Garth. I'm not a psychiatrist. But that was full blown terror I saw in her eyes. Not a small scare. I saw the same look in Karl's eyes at our first Fourth of July fireworks after he came back from the war. He was looking for the nearest foxhole to dive into."

Karl was Ruth's late husband, who had died from lung cancer shortly before I moved to Oakalla.

"It would really help if I could talk to her."

"When she's ready to leave the shelter."

"You'll let me know, then?"

"You'll be the first."

"Thank you." That was something at least, and more than I expected.

The snow, which they now said could total up to four inches, continued to fall at a steady rate of about a half inch an hour. It was a far cry from the worst snow I'd ever seen, but under the circumstances, unexpected and unwanted, one of the most annoying. Long gone were those happy childhood days when I used to pray for snow in order that I might miss a day or so of school and go sledding with my friends, or if no friends appeared, leave my tracks where no one else had been. But I still liked those ferocious storms that growled, whistled, and roared, and shut everything down in their wake. I liked their power and their fury. They made us stop and pay full attention to the natural world around us, whether we wanted to or not, take stock of ourselves and our lives, and be a community again, neighbor helping neighbor—at least until we were all dug out.

But four inches? In Wisconsin? Why bother. There were lots of people around the world who had never seen snow, let alone four inches. Let it go there and make their day.

I dialed Sheriff Stonewall Jackson Huff of Isabella County, Mississippi, and was pleased when my call went through on the first try. Those of us who once had to first call the operator just to make a local call probably would always be somewhat amazed at how much things had changed, would change in our lifetime.

"Sheriff Huff," a deep gruff southern voice said.

"Garth Ryland from Oakalla, Wisconsin. I hope supper's over."

"I just finished a king's portion of grits, greens, and chicken-fried steak, and the best damn red gravy this side of Memphis. Now, I'm about to top a piece of pecan pie with a dip of homemade vanilla ice cream. So you got lucky, I'd say."

"I'll bet it's not snowing there either."

"It's 60, or thereabouts, with every star in the sky showing. Cool by morning, though. I'll need a jacket."

I'd probably need mukluks and parka, but perhaps that was being overly pessimistic. "Trooper Higgins said that you might have some information for me on Orion of Emerald City. Is that right?"

"That might depend on why you're asking. Not that it's a deep dark secret or anything."

I told him about the pickup, Camelia Capers, and Larry Don Loomus. I didn't tell him about the fire at Fickle Store because I didn't want to confuse the issue.

"Yeah, I know Larry Don," he said. "He owns a cattle ranch up in north county. Used to be his daddy's, but since his daddy and mama have both passed on, it's his now."

"I thought he was a private detective from New Orleans?"

"He plays at that, too. Also dabbles in real estate from what I hear. But I thought you were interested in Orion of Emerald City, or am I mistaken?"

I smiled. Good old boys didn't always check in their brains when they put on their badges.

"I'm interested in anything that might tell me what's going on here. If Larry Don Loomus is not what he says he is, I need to know that."

"Be assured, Mr. Ryland, Larry Don is everything he says he is, and more."

"Are you saying he bears watching?"

"No closer than a cottonmouth. You don't shake his cypress tree, I don't think he'll bite. Now, what is that you wanted to know about Orion?"

"For starters, is there such a person?"

"Strange that you should be asking that, since I ask myself that same question almost on a daily basis. Emerald City, you realize, is not an American original. The Wizard of Oz was the first to live there."

"You know, I'd forgotten," I said, ashamed to admit it.

"Easy enough to do, I suppose. Throw in the name Orion and a whole bunch of people running around in white togas, and you can see why I have a hard time taking the whole thing seriously, why I'd like to write them off as a bunch of kooks, since I have not one shred of evidence that there's anything unlawful going on there."

"But . . ." I said, thinking that there was more to the story.

"But on the other hand, there's the matter of that DEA agent they planted in there and was never heard from again."

"DEA agent? I thought Emerald City was a cult."

"The next thing to it anyway."

"Then why not Alcohol, Tobacco, and Firearms?"

There was a pause while, I assumed, he took a bite of his pecan pie a la mode. Those were the days—when Ruth had time to bake, and at this time of year we had pumpkin pie at least once a week, and a fresh fruit pie in every season, including gooseberry, loganberry, and huckleberry.

"I've got a proposition here that can't wait," he said as way of an apology.

"Take all the time you need."

"You, sir, are a scholar and a gentleman."

While I waited for him to finish, I watched the snow as it swooped over the eaves past the south window of the dining room. In the right frame of mind, I could sometimes watch it snow for hours on end. This, however, wasn't one of those times.

"To answer your question of why they planted that DEA agent there, I don't know. The feds are usually pretty closemouthed about what they're up to anyway, and the last person they'd tell is a Mississippi sheriff named Stonewall Jackson Huff, or Jefferson Davis Taylor, as the case may be. My point is, I don't have anything on Orion, even if I might want to."

"Do you want to?"

"That's where it gets sticky. Hate cults. Flat out hate them for all of the mind bending they do. But to be fair, this one seems to do some good. They even take in the homeless, no questions asked."

"And when the homeless want to leave?"

"It's my understanding there's never been a problem with that, either staying or going."

"What about Orion? Earlier you said you weren't sure he even existed. Have you never talked to the man in person?"

"Talked to the man that claimed to be him. A tall skinny blonde with a big head of hair, but wiry, like he could pick cotton all day and never break a sweat. And familiar to me, though I can't place him."

"How old a man?"

"Somewhere between 25 and 40, I'd say. Some men live harder and age faster than others. He appears to be one of them."

"His agenda, if he has one?"

"Asceticism, I believe the name of it is. Less is more.

Simpler is better. Your body is a temple. Don't pollute it. That sort of thing. Far cry from the wine, women, and song that you and I grew up on."

I smiled at his observation, which was dead on. "Does he practice what he preaches?"

"He seems to. And as hard as it is for me to admit, I have to respect him for it. And one on one, I even sort of like the man."

"Then if he's an ascetic, there's no reason for him to have a large sum of money on hand."

Suddenly all was quiet behind me. I turned to discover that Ruth had momentarily quit washing dishes.

"I wouldn't go that far. For those who can afford it, Emerald City costs a pretty penny."

"But if he has no use for it, what does Orion do with the money?"

"Buys more land, builds more buildings, hires more help."

"Isn't that expensive?"

"It didn't use to be. All there was around him was canebrake and worn out cotton fields that nobody else wanted. Of course, the more he buys, the less land there is for everybody else, and the price naturally goes up. He's been good for the economy of Isabella County, if nothing else."

"And Camelia Capers, is her last known address Emerald City?"

"That's where her mother in Hattiesburg keeps sending the checks."

"What does Orion have to say about her?"

"How did you know I asked?"

"Lucky guess."

"I'll bet," he said with a chuckle. "Orion says he hasn't seen nor heard from Miss Capers in over two years now."

"Then why did he hire Larry Don Loomus to find her?"

"He didn't, according to him. He has no knowledge of a person named Larry Don Loomus."

"Do you believe him?"

"It's hard to know what to believe. Emily Capers, Camilla's mother, faxed me a copy of her last cancelled check to Emerald City. It was dated September of this year. So it would seem, at the very least, Mr. Orion has misrepresented the facts of the matter."

"Why would he lie about something like that, when it's so easily proven?"

"That, sir, is a puzzle I'm counting on you to solve."

Neither of us spoke for a moment. Then I said, "Don't take this personally, but how many Stonewall Jackson Huffs are there in Mississippi these days?"

"I'm the only one I know of."

"A true American original."

"I like to think so. I'll be waiting to hear from you, so don't y'all disappoint me now."

I hung up thinking that I was glad that Sheriff Stonewall Jackson Huff and I were on the same side of the law.

"Well?" Ruth said when she could no longer stand it.

"We're at the tip of an iceberg."

"Is Camelia Capers at the center of the iceberg?"

"I'm afraid so, yes."

"Is she in any immediate danger?"

"I don't know, Ruth. If she stole a large sum of money from Orion, as Larry Don Loomus claims, he could have a whole army of people out looking for her scalp."

"You're forgetting one thing," Ruth said. "Only one of them, Larry Don, has shown up here. So either he and Orion have a deal, as Larry Don says, or Larry Don has his own axe to grind."

"Or Orion has sent him as a sacrificial lamb and doesn't plan for either Camelia or Larry Don to make it back to Mississippi alive."

She drained her dishwater and rinsed off her hands before drying them on one of the two tea towels that hung at the end of the counter. "Larry Don Loomis doesn't sound like anyone's sacrificial lamb," she said.

"Agreed."

"So how do you plan to separate the sheep from the goats?"

"I'll call Clarkie."

"Good idea," was her surprising answer.

Harold Clark, or "Clarkie" as he was known in Oakalla, had been chief deputy sheriff under Rupert Roberts, then later sheriff after Whitey Huffer, Rupert's successor, committed suicide. A round, serious, (at first glance) bland man, Clarkie was a computer genius now employed by the Madison Police Force as a computer cop. Under Rupert's guidance, he had been a good deputy, but was a failure as sheriff because he lacked the street smarts and people skills necessary for the job. As a computer cop for the Madison Police Force, he was a complete unabashed success and my first choice whenever I reached a dead end.

I hated to ask him for favors because while he was sheriff I was his chief (sometimes only) supporter and (outside of Ruth) often his harshest critic. Largely at my insistence, he had taken the job in Madison, and while he was happy in his work, and it showed, I felt more than a twinge of guilt every time I came begging at his door. I didn't mind the begging as much as his cheerful acquiescence to my every request. Just once I wanted him to tell me to shove it.

"Clarkie," I said. "It's Garth here."

"Garth! It's been months, it seems."

"August, if I remember right. You sound better now than then. Are things going okay there?"

"They couldn't be better. I took some flak here over that last deal of ours, but it also helped to clear the air. I'm where I belong, even though there are days when I miss Oakalla like crazy. Like tonight, for instance. Instead of sitting at home with my computer, Sheriff Roberts and I would be pulling people out of ditches. You know. *Really* helping real people."

"There's something to be said for that. There's something to be said for what you do, too, especially since you're so good at it."

"You need a favor, right?"

"How did you know?"

"You always need a favor when you call."

I hung my head in shame. "You can always say no, Clarkie."

"What would be the point in that? That wouldn't make either one of us happy. So what do you need?"

"It's a stretch. I'm not sure it's even within *your* realm. But there's a man who calls himself Orion, who resides in Emerald City, Mississippi that I need the lowdown on. Emerald City is not really a city, but a place that may or may not be a cult in Isabella County."

"What do you want to know about him?"

"Everything that you can find out. It would also help me to know whether Emerald City has been cashing Emily Capers' checks, or doing something else with them."

"In whose name?"

"Camelia Capers. She's Emily's daughter, and they're both from Hattiesburg, Mississippi. Camelia is a past resident of Emerald City, who has turned up here in Oakalla. Orion claims that she's been gone from there for at least two years, but her mother claims she's still paying for Camelia, and has the cancelled checks to prove it. It seems that Orion is lying. But what if he isn't?"

"How soon do you need to know?" was all he said.

"Yesterday. Camelia Capers is a bird on a wire. No telling when she might take off."

"I'll get right on it." I was ready to hang up when he said, "I hear Fickle Store burned down Monday night, and they're saying it's arson."

"You heard right. Your aunt Norma call to tell you?"

"No. I saw it on the news here in Madison. Channel 15 had a camera crew out there yesterday."

"Must have been a slow day in the newsroom."

"Arson fires are always big news, Garth. Or haven't you been paying attention?"

"No more than necessary, Clarkie. Good night."

I sat there with my hand still on the receiver. Clarkie had stirred an unpleasant thought with his last comment.

"I heard that crack about Camelia Capers," Ruth said from her chair in the living room.

"I'm not surprised. You heard everything else."

"Do you really think she'll fly the coop the first chance she gets?"

"Yes, Ruth. I really do."

"Then why not let her go, become someone else's problem?"

"Because I don't think she'll get that far."

"Larry Don?"

"Yes. He strikes me as a man who hates to lose at anything."

"Then he's in good company."

"Meaning me, of course."

"Who else would I mean?"

I stood at the window watching the snow. A marvel of consistency, it had already completely covered the ground between us and the neighbors next door.

"Is something else bothering you?" She laid down the magazine that she was pretending to read.

"Something Clarkie said about arson fires being big news. I was thinking that this would be a hell of a night for a fire."

"No worse than any other night."

"You don't have an opinion on the matter?" Although she claimed not to be, Ruth was sometimes psychic.

"I just gave you my opinion. There is no such thing as a good night for a fire."

"That wasn't what I meant."

"I know what you meant."

"Then tell me not to worry."

Ruth sighed in exasperation and went back to her magazine. I stood at the window for a few minutes longer, then put on my coat, gloves, and stocking cap, and went outside.

Chapter 10

The fire siren rang. I jerked awake, not knowing where I was. Then I remembered that I was in my office at the *Oakalla Reporter*. I must have fallen asleep while proofing the local events column for that week's paper. Was it my fault that none of us were leading lives of quiet desperation?

Outside, it sounded like a riot had broken out uptown. The fire siren continued to wail and was soon joined by the sirens of the fire trucks as they left the City Building. Next came the honking of horns amidst the howling of dogs—a fearsome din feeding upon itself, growing louder with each passing second. Then suddenly there was silence, and I could hear the snow hitting the ground at my feet. Unless it was a false alarm, the fire was in the heart of town.

In my hurry to get to the fire, I almost collided with the figure approaching me on Gas Line Road. At the last instant, she veered to the right, crossed the ditch, and disappeared into a flurry of snow. I guessed it was a she. The tracks she left along the side of the road were considerably smaller than mine and about the size of those that Cecil and I had found at Coon Lake.

The whirring red lights led me south on Perrin Street to the United Methodist Church, where firemen stood like mannequins, axes in hand, hesitant to break out stained glass windows they knew to be irreplaceable. Onlookers, church members and non-members alike, some staring silently, others crying out in shocked disbelief, clogged the sidewalk in front of the church and made it difficult for anyone to get through, while a very few others raced in and out of the church in a heroic attempt to save whatever might be saved in the time they had.

I ran into the vestibule, knowing that it was probably futile, but still wanting to do something. The chapel was to the left, the sanctuary to the right. Already there was fire in the sanctuary, smoke pouring out from under the door.

Groping my way along the wall into the chapel, I encountered two men carrying a pew, then a woman in a bathrobe, trying to wrestle the oak pulpit up the center aisle. The pulpit weighed more than she, but she didn't seem to know that.

"Swap ends with me," I said, moving her aside and tipping the pulpit into my arms.

"Gladly."

We were met at the front door by two firemen dragging a hose on their way to the sanctuary and a frightened teenager in a nightshirt and moccasins, who grabbed the woman by her arm and began dragging all three of us— woman, Garth, and pulpit down the front steps of the church.

"Michelle, let go! I'll be okay," the woman shouted.

"I told you not to go in there. It wasn't worth it," the girl said as she continued to drag us toward the street.

It was then that a sea of hands reached out to us, the pulpit disappeared into their midst, and I found myself back inside the chapel with the woman at my side.

"Garth Ryland," I said.

She wiped a strand of hair out of her eyes and offered me her hand. It felt small and slick in mine. I had to hang on tight to keep it from slipping away.

"Janie Gustavson. I'm the pastor here."

"I know. What's left to save . . . besides my soul?"

Her smile said it was probably beyond saving, but she might like to try. "Let's grab as many hymnals as we can. We're probably going to need them."

We were then joined by the same angry teenager who had dragged us down the steps. "Mom, damn it, you're determined to kill yourself, aren't you?"

Reverend Janie Gustavson said nothing. She was too busy racing along the pews gathering hymnals.

"Shut up and help," I said to the girl. "Then we'll all get out of here."

Her face registered shock as her eyes filled with tears. She wasn't used to being talked to that way. But it had its effect. She shut up and helped.

Staggering under our loads, we each carried a stack of hymnals out into the street and had started back inside along with several other people, when we were stopped by Fire Chief Danny Palmer. "I'm sorry, Garth. You can't go back in there. It's too dangerous."

"You see!" the girl shouted at her mother, triumphantly it seemed.

A pretty girl with starkly intelligent eyes, she'd probably had her own way in life until now; and all things being equal, likely would continue to have her own way.

"I can't just stand here and watch," Reverend Janie Gustavson said.

Danny wasn't moved by her entreaty. He'd fought too many fires in the past not to know their danger.

"I'm sorry. That's all you can do. You're not dressed to fight a fire." He looked from her to me. "Either one of you."

"Danny!" one of his firemen yelled.

And he was off and running.

I put my coat around Janie Gustavson, who was starting to shiver in spite of herself, and went in search of a fireman's coat. It was then that I noticed Larry Don Loomus surveying the crowd with an anxious look on his face. His eyes met mine. He gave a cursory nod and continued his search of the crowd. Was he looking for Camelia Capers? If so, I'd better pay attention. But the next time I glanced his way, he was gone.

"Garth, if you're not busy, I could use some help directing traffic," Cecil said.

"I'd rather fight the fire."

He handed me a flashlight with a red lens. "I'm not asking." Then he was off on his own mission.

Eventually I did get my chance to fight the fire, but that was much later after some of the firemen had been overcome with smoke, and they needed a mop-up crew to go into the church to make sure the fire was out. It was out all right. I saw black puddles in the water-soaked carpet, charred pews, broken windows, lights dangling, smoke curling around the remains of what was once an altar, snow sifting in through the holes in the roof, but no fire.

The sad irony was that the building still stood. Its brick and mortar still held fast; there were still a bell and a steeple. But the church was gone, as surely as the life from that cold marbled form that was once your beloved.

"Not a pretty sight, is it?" Danny Palmer had joined me in the sanctuary.

I just stood there in my black rubber coat and yellow plastic hat feeling a loss I couldn't explain. For one of the very few times in my adult life, I cried.

The last hose had been rolled and the last fire truck had left. I was sitting on the curb not feeling the cold when someone put a coat around my shoulders, and a soft warm pair of hands lingered momentarily on my neck.

"Thank you," Reverend Janie Gustavson said.

I glanced up into her sooty tear-streaked face. It was not hard to see where her daughter got her beauty.

"You okay?" I said.

She nodded.

"How about Michelle?"

"I sent her home to bed a few minutes ago." She stared at me a moment longer, then sadly shook her head.

"What?" I said, thinking that perhaps I'd done something wrong.

"Nothing. Sometimes grace comes too late to save us. That's all."

She left in the direction of the parsonage, which was the first house west of the church. I noted that the double row of Lombardy poplars, which separated the church-yard from that of the parsonage and which I had never liked much anyway, had survived the fire. I also noted, by virtue of her bloody footprints, that Reverend Janie Gustavson had somehow lost one of her shoes.

Ruth met me at the front door of the shelter. Somehow I knew she'd be there and likewise knew that I'd have to go through her to get inside.

"I need to talk to Camelia," I said.

"You can't. She's not here," she added before I could protest.

"When did she leave?"

"Liddy doesn't know. She was awakened by the fire

alarm and the next thing she heard was the back door open and close. She went immediately up to Camelia's room and she was gone."

"I told you something like this might happen," I said, as angry at Ruth as I'd ever been.

"So you did. But that doesn't change anything."

"The hell it doesn't! My church just burned down!" I threw up my hands in frustration, not knowing the source of my anger or why it was directed at Ruth.

"It's my church, too, Garth. Don't forget that."

"But Camelia Capers was your charge. And for the life of me I can't figure out why she had the right to go burn our church down just because she was your charge. And why we let her."

"You don't know she burned the church down, Garth. As to why she had the right to stay here in peace, that's what this shelter is for, to protect those who need protecting—from you or anyone else who might do them harm. And regardless of how bad it looks for her, you have no more right to blame Camelia for the fire tonight than you do that woman minister of ours, who, the last time I looked, was nuzzling the collar of your coat."

"Don't change the subject," I said. "No matter what you say, had someone been watching Camelia a little more closely tonight, we at least would know her involvement."

"Point well taken. Now, are you ready to go home? Because I am."

I shook my head no. I wasn't yet ready to make my peace with her.

She locked the front door of the shelter on her way outside. "I'll leave a light on," she said, suddenly sounding weary.

"It didn't have to happen, Ruth."

"No. But it did."

She stepped around me on her way down the steps. I fought the urge to hurry after her and get in step, like a dutiful son. She wasn't to blame for what had happened anymore than I was. She knew that and knew that I knew that. But I had to be angry at someone and it might as well be her.

CHAPTER 11

I awakened long before my alarm ever sounded, dressed, and went downstairs to eat a bowl of Honey Nut Cheerios and drink a glass of orange juice. I'd showered after my arrival home to wash the smoke smell off of me, and my day-old beard fit my mood, so I left it. I wanted to get to the Corner Bar and Grill before the media circus hit town. Today Oakalla would make all the stations in Madison, and if it was a slow news day, some of those in Milwaukee and Chicago. If someone had died in the fire, we probably would have made the national news, so I should have been thankful for small favors.

But I wasn't looking for small favors. I resented anything that disrupted the peace of Oakalla, or cast it in a bad light. Its criticism was my job—as someone who loved it, understood its vagaries, and ultimately forgave them. Small towns only made the news when we burned our churches, or fired our mayors for taking bribes, or murdered our parents as they lay sleeping in bed. Otherwise, we were invisible—a quaint place to visit, but you certainly wouldn't want to live there.

Fair enough, I suppose. News was news, and you had to go where it was happening, or you weren't doing your job. Yet, never once after moving to Oakalla had I gone to a city and, with my camera at the ready, knocked on the door of tragedy to ask those inside how they felt. Was it too much, as a citizen of a small town, to expect the same courtesy?

———————

Shortly after I arrived at the Corner Bar and Grill, Larry Don Loomus joined me at the lunch counter. He'd traded in his designer jeans and leather jacket for Carhart overalls and a hooded denim coat. And like me, he didn't appear to have gotten much sleep lately.

"What are you drinking?" I said.

"Coffee. The same as you."

I ordered him a cup, and waited while he took off his watch cap and unzipped his coat.

"You find Camelia Capers?" I said.

"No. Did you?"

"No, I'm sorry to say."

"That makes two of us."

Bernice brought him a cup of coffee and refilled my cup. "I talked to Orion yesterday," I said, bending the

111

truth a little. "He claims he's never heard of you, or seen anything of Camelia Capers for the past two years."

Larry Don did not take that news well. "Pardon my French, sir, but Mr. Orion is a goddamn liar if he told you that, and you can tell him I said so."

"Why would he lie about something like that?"

"I'm sure he has his reasons." Larry Don rose from his stool without touching his coffee. "Now if you'll excuse me . . ."

"Camelia Capers," I said, not wanting him to get away before I had a chance to talk to him. "Do you think she could have set the fire last night?"

"For what possible reason?"

I couldn't tell him without involving the shelter. "Who knows. I just wondered if she had it in her?"

"Camelia Capers is a lot of things, but I don't think she's a firebug."

"You *are* familiar with her background, then?" At our first meeting he had feigned ignorance on the subject.

Larry Don's eyes were as cold as the day outside. "Mr. Orion filled me in during our last communication, another fact that he no doubt has conveniently overlooked."

"Do you think he's had a change of heart about her and is trying to cut his losses?"

"I don't know what his game is. But it is my immediate intention to find out."

I nodded in the direction of the barroom. "There's a pay phone in there just to the right of where we were sitting yesterday."

He put on his watch cap and zipped up his jacket. "A private matter, sir, between Mr. Orion and me." Then he left.

When Bernice came back to the counter to refill my cup for a second time, she noticed that Larry Don had not drunk his coffee. "Is there something wrong with the coffee, Garth? I just made a fresh pot."

"No, the coffee's fine. Mr. Loomus decided that there was someplace else he needed to be."

"Like everyone else lately," she said with resignation. "Speaking of which, Beezer hasn't made an appearance since we last talked."

I took one last sip of coffee and dropped a couple dollars on the counter. "I'll be headed out that way soon."

"I wish you'd gone yesterday when I first mentioned it."

"I did. Beezer wasn't there."

"Oh." She was sorry to hear that. "Have you heard what started the fire at the church last night?"

"No. That's my next stop."

"The word I got was that it was set, just like Fickle Store."

I slid off the stool and hit the floor with a jolt. Nothing like cold dead feet to remind you when you've reached 50.

"Was Hiram still here when the fire started last night?" I said.

"No. Because of the weather he closed up early. He was already home and on his way to bed."

No help there, I decided. I said, "If Beezer does happen to show up here, whatever the hour or circumstances, I want either you or Hiram to let me know."

"Do you really think he will show up here again?"

113

"I'm counting on it," I lied. No point in ruining both our days.

The day had yet to dawn, but already had showed its hand. The wind persisted out of the northwest and had a damp bite to it. The clouds lay flat and still, like a low gray ceiling atop Oakalla's street lights. Nowhere did I see any sign of moon, stars, sun, or sky, or of anything else that might give me hope for a break in our fortune. We were locked in gloom, as surely as if someone had stuffed us into a closet and turned the key.

Danny Palmer was alone in the Marathon. His eyes were bloodshot and his face wore the shadow of fatigue. He sat at his desk the way that I had sat at mine late last night, too tired to move and too bleary to think and too stubborn to give up and go home to bed.

"A penny for your thoughts," I said.

"If I had any."

I pulled up a stool and sat beside him. "You'd better find some. I predict that within the hour a whole bunch of people are going to come calling."

Danny yawned, laid his head down on his desk. "I know and I'm dreading it."

"Was it arson?" I said.

"As near as I can tell. The fire seems to have started in the closet at the back of the sanctuary where the choir keeps their robes. I found a burned-out two-gallon gas can in the sanctuary."

"Just like Fickle Store."

Danny forced himself to lift his head and open his eyes. "And the cabin on Coon Lake."

"Has anybody stopped by lately to fill up their two-gallon gas cans?"

"Nobody I know of. I asked Sniffy and he said he didn't remember anybody either. Of course in summer it happens on almost a daily basis, and any time of year there's always somebody in here buying gas for his chainsaw."

"But not lately?"

"Not that I recall."

"What about the hardware? Fritz had a run on two-gallon gas cans of late?"

"He says not."

"Why would someone advertise the fact that it was arson? It almost seems like they don't care if we know."

"That's what I've been sitting here trying to figure out," Danny said as he absent-mindedly leafed through the stack of invoices on his desk. "Advertise is the word I came up with. It seems to me that they *want* us to know it's arson."

"To what end?"

"That's what I can't figure out. But I'm fairly certain the same person started both fires, and maybe that one two years ago over on Coon Lake. I've never let it be known about the gas cans I found, so it can't be a copycat."

"Cecil knew about the gas can."

"So did you. But I'm hoping neither one of you told anyone else."

"What about the state fire marshal? Does he know about the gas cans?"

"He knows about the one at Fickle Store. He'll soon know about the others. I hear he's paying us another visit, along with the FBI."

"Why the FBI?"

"It was a church, remember? Hate crimes and all that."

"Do we know it was a hate crime?"

"I don't know what else you'd call it."

"Maybe a crime of opportunity."

He shrugged. "That's for somebody else to figure out. I'm just glad I make my living pumping gas."

"I wouldn't say that too loudly. Somebody might not see the humor," I said as the phone rang.

"Thanks for reminding me," Danny said as he reached across his desk to answer the phone.

"What are friends for?"

It was a lonely walk out to Beezer's cabin. I met no cars on their way into town; saw no recent tracks in the snow where a car had been. I did hear the whistle of duck wings as a flock passed by overhead on their way south, but there in the middle of Gas Line Road with only the snow for company, that made me feel even more alone.

No one was home at Beezer's. The dusting of snow on

the seat of his Moped had grown to about five inches, and the iron wagon wheel was all but buried in a drift of snow. Inside, the cabin had the same semblance of warmth as the day before, but when I checked the wood stove, I again found no live coals.

There appeared to be remnants of tracks leading from Beezer's back door, but when I tried to follow them, I soon found myself doing more guessing than tracking. When they didn't appear to lead in the direction that I wanted to go, I gave up and headed for the corncrib where the pickup was parked.

But I knew in my bones that it would be gone when I got there. Even if Camelia hadn't started the fire as a diversion to help her escape, she surely would have used that opportunity when it presented itself. Or at least she would have tried. The hill to the west of the corncrib would be formidable under the best of conditions, and might prove impossible to climb in the snow.

This shows how much I knew. The pickup was still there in the corncrib with Old Elmo's head on its hood and no indication that either had been moved.

Then I noticed tracks in the snow that I'd missed on my way to the corncrib. They appeared to have been made in the night after most of the snow had fallen, and led up the hill west of the corncrib. At the top of the hill I was surprised when they led south, instead of north toward Gas Line Road.

They continued in a straight line to the end of the alfalfa field and into the woods again, where it got harder for me to follow them after they hit a well- trodden deer path and jumped off into a thick stand of cedars. I lost them in the cedars, but found them again when they crossed a woven wire fence and started up the steep grade toward the railroad tracks.

But a train had already been by that morning, and whoever I was following had been clever enough and agile enough to walk the rails when he reached them. I assumed it was a man because the tracks were larger than mine.

With no footprints to tell me which way to go, and remembering that Hattie Peeler said that the pickup went east when it left the alfalfa field, I went east along the railroad in the hope of finding the tracks again. About a mile later I gave up. Despite the cold, I'd started to sweat and was growing more weary and discouraged with every step. Adding to my misery was the thought of having to retrace every new step I'd take, and every old step I'd taken.

I turned around. About halfway back to my starting point I noticed the faint smell of wood smoke. It couldn't be coming from Beezer's cabin because there was no fire in the stove, and it shouldn't be coming from anywhere to the north of that because there were no dwellings for a couple miles, so it had to be coming from the woods in between.

I climbed the fence at the bottom of the railroad grade, crossed the south end of somebody's corn field, and entered the woods, which was crisscrossed by a series of small ravines, all leading back toward the creek that ran through Beezer's property. It was by accident that I discovered the pile of brush at the end of one of the ravines, where someone had been living of late. The brush had been hollowed out beyond its narrow opening and inside was a deep bed of pine boughs that, I assumed, no beaver had chiseled from the nearby trees.

Yet I could find no discernible human tracks either leading to the lair or away from it. There were some squirrel tracks in the area and what appeared to be those of a fox, but they told me nothing I needed to know.

On the move again, I followed the smoke to a small clearing where I found the coals of a campfire and what I took for the bones of Old Elmo. Old Elmo's hindquarters hung from a pine bough at the edge of the clearing and were being hacked away and eaten as needed.

No human footprints were there either. The fire had been a small one, so it couldn't have been burning all night, but when I made a full circle of the clearing, I found nothing that told me which way to go. Puzzled, and without direction, I decided to go back to Oakalla.

Chapter 12

I was nearing my office when Cecil met me in his patrol car. "Now you show up," I said as I climbed inside.

Cecil turned around in the park and drove to my office. I was hot and sweaty after my long hike. Cecil wore an angry, pensive look. Neither one of us would have won a congeniality contest.

"You on your way back from Beezer's?" he said.

"Yes. He's not there."

"Didn't figure he would be, but I was on my way out there myself. You see all those books of his while you were there?"

"They're hard to miss," I said, leaning my head back against the seat and closing my eyes. Now that I was back in the warm again, I was suddenly sleepy.

"What do you figure he does with all of them?"

"Reads them would be my first guess. I remember someone once telling me that when he lived up north,

Beezer spent most of his winter days in bed reading books." I made myself sit up and put my hand on the latch, but I couldn't yet force myself to open the door and start what promised to be an endless day of work.

"Garth, I have a favor," he said. "I want you to talk to Michelle Gustavson for me."

"Why?"

"Because she's the one who called in the fire last night. I talked to her this morning at school, but didn't get anywhere with her, maybe because I didn't ask the right questions."

"You don't think she told you the truth?"

"I don't know what to think of her, Garth. That's why I'm asking for a second opinion."

I gave a silent groan. I really didn't want to do it. In the first place, I wasn't sure how well I liked the girl, or more to the point, how well she liked me. In the second place, I didn't have time. "It will have to wait until this afternoon," I said. "I haven't even started my column yet."

"I don't care as long as it's done before Friday night."

"Why Friday night?"

"These fires seem to be coming in twos, Garth. Two fires two days apart with a two-gallon gas can at each. Two days from last night will be Friday night."

"That will make three fires," I said.

He chose to ignore the observation. "Not if I have anything to say about it. Which is why I plan to be on patrol from dusk until dawn."

"For how long?"

"For however long it takes to put a stop to them."

"As Grandmother Ryland said about my first muskey and my prospects for a second, that could be ten minutes or ten years from now. We don't even know that last night's fire wasn't the last."

His jaw was set, his pale blue eyes in sharp focus. "However long it takes, Garth. I mean that."

"Who'll be out there during the day in your absence?" I said.

"Hell, Garth, cops from all over, including the FBI, are going to be in and out of here the next few days. We won't need anybody else."

"Until they decide to leave."

"I'll cross that bridge when I have to."

I opened the door of the Impala and that was as far as I got. The air rushing in was a whole lot colder than the air leaking out.

"You ever get back over to Fickle to talk to Jasper, or to White Lick to talk to Carl Bolin?" I said.

"No. I never made it that far yesterday. I figure it's up to you now."

"I'm not sure they'll leave it up to me, Cecil."

"Who's that, Garth?"

"The state police. If not them, the FBI. Not with a task force that's been in place for the past few years now."

"But you will talk to Michelle Gustavson this afternoon?" If not, I was about to be persuaded.

"I'll talk to her. But don't be surprised if it lands us

122

both in hot water. We're persona non grata—in the eyes of everyone about to be involved here."

"Whatever we are, you still get my vote."

I stepped outside and closed the door. Cecil sat there for a moment as if unsure of his direction, then put the Impala in gear, backed out into Berry Street, and took off for home. Maybe he'd decided against talking to anyone about the fire on general principles, or maybe he figured he needed his sleep more than they needed his opinion. Whatever the case, I wished I could have joined him.

I spent the rest of the morning drinking instant coffee and working on the paper, but deliberately left my column until evening. Sometimes I wrote better under pressure. Sometimes I didn't have a clue about what I was going to say until I started. Sometimes the subject was so large and personal that I was afraid to approach it until I absolutely had to—which was the case this time.

When the noon siren rang, I jumped out of my chair and was already at the coat rack when I realized that it wasn't a fire. Having gone that far, I decided that I might as well continue on up to the Corner Bar and Grill for lunch.

A couple blocks up Gas Line Road I decided to take a last minute detour to see what I might find there in the vacant lot between Gas Line Road and Junior Derflinger's house. A lot of mice runs it turned out, but not much else.

When I reached what used to be Doc Airhart's back yard, now the back yard of the shelter, I paused over a trail of footprints that seemed to lead from the shelter on an angle toward Gas Line Road. Not far from their path were the remnants of the orchard where Doc Cook used to keep his beehives, which still was home to one broken super and a few scraggly apple trees that despite the odds were over laden with fruit every year. I began to follow the footprints back toward their source.

They ended at the back door of the shelter without any side trips along the way. They also appeared to belong to a tall woman with a long stride, who was in a hurry to get wherever she was going.

I went around the shelter without going inside and was on my way to the Corner Bar and Grill when I saw a lone figure staring into the remains of the United Methodist Church. Even if I hadn't been looking for her, I would have recognized her immediately.

Reverend Janie Gustavson had come to Oakalla in June, following her appointment by the South Central Wisconsin Conference of the United Methodist Church. Because of their circuit-rider tradition, once rooted in evangelical fervor, United Methodist ministers tended to change churches more often than those of other established churches. And those who came to Oakalla tended to stay a shorter time than, say, at First Church Madison, because when you arrived at a small stable church like Oakalla, you were either on your way up, or on your way down, or had never gotten very far to begin with. If you were good and the church prospered, you went on to larger, greener pastures. If you were bad and the church floundered, you usually left the ministry and took a job in social services. If you were mediocre and the church limped along as it always had, you usually stayed until you wore out your welcome, or retired, as was often the case.

Where Janie Gustavson fit in that mix, I didn't know. With her short straight chestnut hair, emerald green eyes, and strong sleek track runner figure, she was attractive enough to get me inside the church to listen to one of her sermons just to see what she was made of. I came away with a feeling of sadness and regret because although I liked her as a person, I expected more from her sermon than I got. Probably not her fault, I decided in retrospect, since it had been nearly 30 years since I *had* been moved by a sermon. So I went back a couple times more, with the same result.

After the third time, I said never again. On each occasion I had wanted to come away, if not enlightened, or refreshed, at least feeling that I had seen a rising star in action. Instead, I came home, fixed myself an Old Crow and ginger ale, and had a buzz on by noon.

"You hungry? I'm buying if you are," I said to her.

She wore a long tweed coat that nearly dragged the ground and her hands were stuffed into its wide deep pockets. "Is it Garth Ryland who's asking?" she said without turning around.

"One in the same."

"Then yes, I am hungry."

I locked her arm in mine and we started up Madison

Road toward the Corner Bar and Grill. "Where did all the people go, or haven't they gotten here yet?" I said.

"You'll find out."

I did find out. The Corner Bar and Grill was packed, with even some people standing and waiting for either a booth to open up, or a seat at the lunch counter. A camera crew was shooting a young reporter's interview with Dub Bennett and Sniffy Smith, who each wore a guru-like expression of wisdom as they fed her the same pap that they'd been feeding us for years, and she bought every word of it.

I made us a path through the lunchroom into the barroom. The only seats available were the two at the north end of the bar. We took them.

"I don't think I've ever sat at a bar before," Janie Gustavson said.

I took her coat and mine and carried them into the back room where I laid them on top of the euchre table. "Not even in college?" I said on my return.

"Preachers' kids don't sit at bars. Or at least they didn't used to."

"Preachers either, that I recall."

"Any port in a storm."

"That's what I've always said."

Then there was an awkward moment of silence, but it soon passed.

"Haven't seen you in church lately," she said, being nice about it. "Except for last night, of course."

I grabbed two menus from behind the bar, handing

one of them to her. "I haven't been to church lately. It's not something that I do much anymore," I said.

"That's good. I thought maybe it was me."

Janie Gustavson wore jeans, an off-white turtleneck sweater, and red lipstick. There was a hint of blush to her cheeks and a hint of sadness in her eyes.

"No. It's not you, it's me," I said, wishing that we were talking about anything else. "I can't say I've lost my faith, but I can't say I haven't either."

"Yet there you were, helping out last night."

"Losing my faith is one thing. Losing my church is something else again."

Tears came into her eyes as she tried to read the menu. "Tell me about it." She handed the menu back to me. "I give up. What's good here?"

"How hungry are you?"

"Not very."

"The fish sandwiches are always good. If you like salad, the lettuce is usually fresh."

"Then I'll have a fish sandwich with a side of tossed salad."

"What to drink?"

"What are you drinking?"

I had the feeling that if I'd said a beer, she would have had one right along with me. "Iced tea. Otherwise, I won't get any work done this afternoon."

She smiled, looked relieved. "I'll have iced tea, too, then."

When Hiram came to take our order, he looked

harried and frustrated. Occasionally he came in to help out with noon meals whenever there was an auction in town or Bernice was otherwise expecting a big crowd, but he'd never learned to like it. Hiram preferred leisurely nights and his regular crowd.

"What'll you have, Garth?"

I ordered beef-and-noodles, the lunch special.

"And the lady?"

I told him.

"Sorry to be in such a rush," he said as he jotted it down. "But I'm six orders behind the way it is."

"Just don't run out of beef-and-noodles in the meantime."

"Wish I could promise that," he said, as he hurried off to the kitchen.

I watched Janie Gustavson slowly survey the barroom, wondering what she thought of it all, here among us heathens. Above the bar, the Hamms bear continued to roll the same log that he'd been rolling for the past couple decades or so, and there in the middle of the barroom was the jukebox filled with country records that nobody was playing because you couldn't hear for all of the noise. The floor of the barroom was yellow poplar, the walls knotty pine. There were five tables, six booths, all of them filled, and a mirror that ran the length of the bar. Swinging doors led to the lunchroom, and a wide wooden stairway without railings led down to the restrooms, and the cellar where Hiram kept his wine and kegs of beer. Not in the least bit pretentious, and from cellar to ceiling, my kind of place.

"I like it here. I wish I'd come in here sooner," Janie said.

"I'm not sure the church board would concur with that decision," I said.

"No," she said, letting her hand rest against mine. "But Jesus would." When I raised my brows at that, she said, "Where else to find all the sinners?"

"Sunday morning in church," I said, not to be outdone.

"Amen" was all she said. Although I did notice that she took her hand away.

"So," I said to break the silence a few seconds later, "what's a nice girl like you doing in a place like this?"

"It's a long story," she said, not wanting to talk about it.

"It looks like we have time."

"Let's turn it around then. What's a nice guy like you doing in a place like this?" she said.

"Don't you read my newspaper?"

"I quit after you stopped listening to my sermons."

"That's fair enough, I suppose."

"Not really, but that's the way I am."

Hiram brought us our iced tea. I wished then that I'd ordered a beer. I might need it to get through this.

I said, "To answer your question, I came here several years ago from the *Milwaukee Journal* because my grandmother Ryland died, leaving me her small farm northwest of town and enough money to buy the *Oakalla Reporter*, something that I'd always wanted to do. I was recently divorced and our only child, a son, had died a few months before, so pulling up stakes and starting over was no problem. In fact, it was almost a necessity by then. I came here, bought a house, found a housekeeper who made my house her own, and have been here ever since. I love Oakalla, though I don't always like it, and if it can keep its people and its heart, I plan to spend the rest of my life here, however long or short that may be."

"No significant others in your life?" she said.

"Not counting Ruth and Jessie?" I said with a smile.

"Ruth, I know. I've seen her in church a time or two, and visited with her at the shelter. But who's Jessie?"

"My car. But that's another tale altogether."

"You still didn't answer my question."

"Yes. I have someone. We have each other, I think. As to whether I can say that a year from now, the jury is still out."

"Why is that?"

"She's in Detroit for the time being. She's not exactly sure that she will be returning to Oakalla, although she's starting to lean that way."

"And you're willing to wait in the meantime?"

"Willing is not the word I'd use. But yes, I'll wait in the meantime."

"She's a lucky woman," she said, touching her hand to mine before withdrawing it again. "Not that I was interested, of course."

"Of course."

I passed our next few moments of silence looking around

the barroom. More cops were in there than media people, I guessed by their pale-faced, button-down appearance. Though it could have been a crew from "Sixty Minutes."

Reverend Janie Gustavson said, "To answer *your* question, I was serving as a supply minister for Centenary in Madison when this appointment came open, so I jumped at the chance. Like you said, a move was not only intriguing, but necessary."

"For whose sake, yours or Michelle's?"

"I'm surprised you remembered her name." For some reason that bothered her, as warning flags went up in those bright green eyes of hers.

"She dragged me down the church steps, if I'm not mistaken."

"For both of our sakes," she said without further comment. "I didn't like some of the friends that Michelle was keeping in Madison, or the hours, and I felt I needed a fresh start away from there."

I waited for her to go on. There was more to the story, I was sure. There always is.

Finding something in my eyes that she didn't like, she looked away. "You see, after nearly 20 years of marriage, my husband left me for another woman. Michelle was devastated. So was I."

"What does your husband do?"

"He was a minister. Though he's since left the ministry."

"Is his name by any chance William Gustavson?" If so, I had listened to many of his sermons.

She seemed to resent the excitement in my voice. "Yes.

His name is William Gustavson. We met while I was a student at the University of Wisconsin, and he was the minister there at University Church. In fact, he was the one who encouraged me to become a minister, though as things turned out, I was always too busy with his ministry to take on a church of my own."

"Until after your divorce."

"Yes. Suddenly I had all the time in the world to do whatever I wanted. Or so it seemed."

Hiram brought us our food. As always when Hiram was serving, it arrived piping hot. I had to blow on my first few bites of beef-and-noodles before I could eat them.

"How has Michelle taken to the move?" I said between bites.

"Not as well as I have. She knows it's for her own good, but that's beside the point. And she still blames me for the divorce, so that's always there between us."

"How can she blame you?"

"Because I'm the easiest target. Most mothers are in these cases."

"But you can't fault her love for you. She followed you into a burning building to make sure you didn't die in there."

Janie Gustavson had eaten half of her sandwich and was picking at her salad. "No. I can't fault that. In spite of everything, we're still each other's best friend."

"Does she see her father on a regular basis?"

"She spent this summer with him in Florida. She'll spend Christmas vacation with him."

She set her salad bowl on top of her sandwich plate

and shoved them both aside. "Do you mind getting my coat for me?"

I retrieved her coat and mine from the back room.

"You don't have to walk me home. I know you're a busy man," she said once we were outside.

"I've got an errand to run anyway."

"Oh? And where's that?"

"The school. I need to talk to Michelle. With your permission?"

"What do you need to talk to her about?"

"The fire. She was an eye witness. It's a favor to Marshal Hardwick."

"Why doesn't he talk to her?"

"He has. He wants a second opinion."

She stopped walking so that I would have to face her in case I thought about lying to her. "Why?"

"Marshal Hardwick hasn't been on the job very long. He's not sure he asked the right questions."

"Why ask her any questions?"

"Because she's the one who called in the fire."

Looking puzzled, she took my arm and we started walking again. "I'm sorry. I didn't know that."

"You weren't awake at the time?"

"No. Michelle is the night owl in the family. I'm the old setting hen. If I'm not in bed by ten every night, I'm wasted the next day."

"Was Michelle at home when you went to bed?"

"Yes. She was in her room listening to music and doing her homework."

"Then is she the one who told you about the fire?"

"No. I was awakened by the siren. When I came out into the hallway, Michelle told me that the church was on fire. I grabbed my robe, put on the first pair of shoes that I could find . . . Well, you know the rest."

We'd reached the parsonage and were standing at the bottom of its front steps. Fired a deep red that was almost black, its bricks rose two stories to dormers that looked out on Church Street. The shortest street in town, Church ran the half block between School Street and Madison Road.

"Here's where I get off," Janie said.

"What now? With the church, I mean?"

"We hold services in the Lutheran Home until we can make arrangements somewhere else."

"What about the church itself? Do you want to rebuild?"

"That's up to the congregation. I'd like to rebuild here, but even if we do, the old church is going to have to come down, or so I was told this morning by the fire marshal. So it probably makes sense to build there west of town where we'll have room to put in an educational unit."

"I figured," I said, feeling my guts start to churn.

"Wouldn't you like a new church?"

"No. The old one suited me just fine."

"But you never went there."

"That's beside the point."

"You can't have your cake and eat it too," she said.

"So I've been told."

Abruptly, she gave me a long hard hug. "Thanks for lunch," she said. "It's exactly what I needed."

"You're easy to please."

Her smile made me think of her as a lot of things, but a minister wasn't one of them. "Try me sometime."

CHAPTER 13

Assistant Principal Caroline May was a hard-as-nails woman of 50 with a slight build, thin, flat, salt-and-pepper hair, and the belief that discipline was not just the order of the day, but the foundation on which all education rested. A former nun whose truck-driver husband still called her Sister Caroline whenever they butted heads, she had been on the job for only a year, but already I could see progress. In the past whenever I was there, the school office resembled the waiting room of a bus station, with about the same decorum. Today all of the people in there belonged there and not one of them was a student.

"Sister Caroline," I said to the school secretary. "She's expecting me."

"Better not let her hear you call her that."

"Call me what?" the question came from Caroline May's office.

"You see," the school secretary said.

Caroline May came out from behind her desk to shake my hand. Hers was a warm dry grip that belied the steel in her bearing. She wore a checked black-and-white suit with white hose and a red silk scarf, and a smile that said that even though she was glad to see me, not to take up too much of her time.

"Have a seat," she said.

I took a seat in the high-backed wooden chair facing hers. The chair matched those in my office for comfort, which is to say it had none.

"Where did you dig this up?" I said in reference to the chair.

"In the closet off the band room. You're the one who gave me the idea."

Before she had taken the job with the school, Caroline May had come to my office to ask me both about the job and Oakalla itself. A city girl all of her life, she wasn't sure either that she would fit in here, or that she was willing to give up all of the amenities that a city like Chicago obviously offered. I told her that she would have no problem fitting in, but as for the amenities that she was used to, Oakalla had next to none. "What could I say to recommend it?" she then asked. I gave her a one word answer: Community. So far she hadn't called me on it.

"You don't have to copy all my bad habits," I said.

"Only those that get results." She walked around me to close her office door. It was time to get down to business. "So, what do you want to know about Michelle?"

"For starters, your general impression of her."

"She's a good kid. Next question."

"What do you mean by a good kid? Is she also a good girl?"

"Yes, to answer your second question. She's a good girl. 'She don't drink and she don't chew, or go out with boys who do.' As far as her being a good kid goes, I like her. Like you, she's smarter than the average bear, but I don't hold that against her."

"Has she ever talked to you about her father?"

"Not in so many words. She's still angry about her folks' divorce, but what kid isn't."

"You've taken her under your wing, haven't you? Is there a reason for that?"

She picked a pencil up off her desk and tossed it my way. I tried to catch it, but succeeded only in knocking it to the floor.

"Nice hands," she said.

"They used to be . . . once upon a time."

"So you say."

In the silence that followed, I could see her mentally reach into her purse for the pack of cigarettes that used to be there. Since she couldn't smoke on school property, she didn't smoke anywhere anymore.

She said, "Okay, I've taken Michelle under my wing. Somebody had to, and I decided it might as well be me. She loves her mother, but worries about her. She loves her father, but there's some kind of barrier between them that she won't talk about. She likes the kids here and they like her, but she doesn't see as much drive and ambition out of them as she would like. Sometimes she feels like a round peg in a square hole. She can make herself fit, but it's not very comfortable."

"What does she plan to do when she graduates?"

"Go to Stetson University. She hasn't decided on a major, but she's leaning toward English. She thinks she might like to be a writer someday."

"Is she a happy kid?"

"As any of us are at that age. For the most part she likes who she is and where she's been, but she's ready to move on."

I stood and offered my hand. "Thanks for your help."

"You're welcome."

Michelle Gustavson had long straight auburn hair brushed until it shone, and she wore a green-and-black plaid wool skirt, white wool sweater, and white knee socks that try though they might, could not quite reach the hem of her skirt, or hide the fact that ankle-to-thigh she had a lovely pair of legs. We were sitting in the counselor's office. I was studying her, amazed at how much she resembled her mother, particularly her eyes. Except for Michelle's hair, which was longer, fuller, and much darker, they were alike in almost every respect.

"What are you staring at?" she said, obviously annoyed at me.

"I was just noting how much you look like your mother. Except for your hair."

"She dyes hers," she said.

I smiled, thinking that it probably was the other way around. "Your mother is a pretty woman. It's a compliment," I said.

"Are you a letch?" she asked me straight out.

"Yes. But I'm not after either you or your mother."

"Too bad. She could use a man in her life."

Since she brought it up, I said, "Why do you say that? I'd think you might want to have her to yourself for a while."

"Once the school year's over, I'm out of here. What's she going to do then?"

"She's a big girl. I'm sure she'll think of something."

"You don't know Mom very well, do you?" she said with a look of scorn. "With no one to come home to, she'll throw herself into her work and end up having a breakdown. You'll see."

"I'd rather not, if it comes to that."

"Then take her out every once in a while. You don't have to love her. Just show her some affection."

I just stared at her until she looked away. "Your mother is not a charity case, Michelle. She's a lovely vibrant woman."

"I know. I'm sorry," she said, looking genuinely contrite. "It's just that she tries so hard and . . . Well, you've heard her preach. What do you think?"

"I'm at a loss for words."

"Right. So am I whenever she asks me about her

sermons. She's not very good, and you and I both know it. My dad, though. He was something else again."

Her whole countenance changed when she spoke of her father. A whole new light came into her eyes, a whole new timbre to her voice. She was her daddy's girl, no question about it.

"I know. I've heard your father preach."

"When?"

"Years ago. I thought then, I do now, he was the best preacher I ever heard."

"Don't let Mom hear you say that, or you won't get to first base with her."

"I'm not trying to get to first base with her, remember?"

"So you say."

"And as for your mother's preaching, it's not fair to compare her to your father. Almost anyone will pale under that light."

"Yeah. That's what I keep telling myself. But no matter how you slice it, she still isn't very good is she? Is she?" she repeated when she saw me start to squirm.

"No."

She clenched her fists and looked up at the ceiling. "Thank you, Lord. Somebody besides me has the guts to admit it."

I looked beyond her to the clock on the wall. School would dismiss before too long. I didn't want to get trampled in the stampede.

"Since I've made your day, do you mind answering a couple questions about the fire last night?" I said.

"No, I don't mind. That's why you're here, isn't it?"

I nodded. "Your mother says that you're a night owl, so that explains why you were still up when the fire started. I guess what I want to know is how you happened to see it?"

"That's easy. I always sleep with my window cracked, even in winter. Mom always closes it after I leave in the morning, and I always have to open it again before I go to bed. I was standing there opening it when I saw something glowing inside the church. A spirit, I thought at first. I'm seeing a miraculous presence of some kind. I stood there for several seconds spellbound by it all, thinking that this surely can't be happening to me. Then I realized what was really going on."

"Did you see anybody leaving the church?"

Her eyes, flawless until then, momentarily clouded. "No. No one I recognized anyway."

"But you did see someone?"

"I can't be sure. You know, when you're home alone at night, how your eyes and ears can play tricks on you if you let them, see and hear things that aren't really there. Well, it could've been a shadow I saw, as well as a man."

"Alone? I thought your mother was there in the parsonage with you."

"You know what I mean. If the other person is locked away in her bedroom, you might as well be alone."

"You're sure it was a man you saw?"

"No. I'm not *sure* I saw anybody. But if I did see somebody, it was a man."

"Going in what direction?"

"What direction is the church from the parsonage?"

"East."

I waited while she used her hands to figure directions. "North, it would have been. Northeast actually."

"Walking or running?"

"Running. Moving swiftly anyway."

"What did you do next?"

"Called in the fire."

"And after that?"

"Stood at my window and watched."

"You didn't think to awaken your mother?"

"I thought about it then gave it up as a bad idea. I knew she'd go running in there, trying to save anything and everything she could. But once the siren rang, there was no stopping her."

"Not because you didn't try."

Michelle Gustavson shook her head at the futility of it. "Mom's an idiot when it comes to things like that. In Madison, we were driving along the Beltline, when we saw this guy jump off a bridge into the lake. She pulled the car off the road and would have gone in after him, if Dad hadn't stopped her. It turned out the guy had a buddy waiting for him in a boat below the bridge. Both of them were stoned out of their minds."

"Better to care too much than too little," I said.

"Yes. But you don't have to be stupid about it. She could have gotten herself killed for nothing."

I studied her momentarily, decided that Michelle

143

Gustavson would never make that mistake. "I'm sorry for yelling at you last night. I didn't realize the circumstances."

"You should be sorry," she said, then added with a smile, "but if I'd known who you were, I wouldn't have worried so much."

"Who I was?"

"The famous Garth Ryland. Mom is always reading your column to me, as if I couldn't read it for myself."

"I thought she quit reading my column after I quit going to church."

"Did she tell you that? And she thinks I don't always tell the truth. Wait until I get home."

"I'd rather you wouldn't say anything to her."

"Why should you care—if you aren't interested in either one of us?" Her eyes, green and mischievous, told me how much she was enjoying herself at my expense.

"Just because," I said.

"I'll think about it."

We neither spoke for a moment. Then I said, "Why English, as a major?"

"Why not English? I know it's not very practical, but then neither am I."

"You don't share your parents' calling?"

"Is that some kind of sick joke? I don't share either their calling or their faith. It's one of the two things Dad and I fight about."

"What's the other?"

"That's my business."

"Then we'll leave it at that. Do you need me to walk you back to your room?"

"I don't need you to, but it would be nice if you would. For an old lech, most of the kids think you're kind of cool."

"I guess that's a compliment."

I walked her through the grade school, along the sleek gray concrete corridor to the high school, then up the stairs to the chemistry room. There she went inside, leaving me to wonder what she hadn't told me.

Chapter 14

While I was in the school, it began snowing again. A thin white haze that fell as tiny beads, it gave the trees along Gas Line Road a haunted loom, and struck an icy cord that started with my toes and ended in my bones.

Still wearing my coat to ward off the chill, I called Ruth at the shelter from my office. The very next thing I planned to do was to fix myself a boiling hot cup of coffee.

"Ruth, this is Garth. I need a favor."

"I suppose under the circumstances I owe you one."

A large one, I thought, but didn't make the mistake of saying so. "There's a former United Methodist minister by the name of William Gustavson. I want you to find out all you can about him."

"Any particular reason why?"

"He's Janie Gustavson's ex-husband, Michelle

Gustavson's father. While I was in college, we used to call him Wild Bill, partly because of his lifestyle and partly because rumor had it that he had once killed a man. But I don't recall the circumstances, if I ever knew them."

"But why him? Why now?"

"I just finished talking to his daughter. She's a bright charming girl, but there's something that's not quite right about her story concerning the fire last night. She said that, though she can't be sure, she thought she saw a man leave the church shortly after the fire started. I don't see how that could be."

"Why couldn't it be?"

I started to explain, but she jumped to her own conclusions.

"Oh I see. It couldn't be a man because Camelia is your one and only suspect."

"Until I can prove otherwise," I said for orneriness sake. I'd tell her the truth only when she'd listen.

"Garth, you're not making any sense. How is getting the lowdown on William Gustavson going to help you find Camelia?"

"Did you ever hear him preach, Ruth?"

"No. I can't say I did."

"Then you missed something special. He had it all— power, delivery, anecdotes, humor, and a brilliant mind to go with it. I want to know what happened to him, why his two fledglings are here in Oakalla with only each other to look after them."

There was a pause. Then she said, "This isn't about the

fire, is it, Garth? And it really could have been a man that Michelle Gustavson saw leaving the fire last night."

Let her believe what she wanted. "Call me when you learn something."

I began to jot down notes for my column, but still made no attempt to write it, because I wasn't yet sure that I was going to write it. I was still afraid that I would do the subject an injustice by broaching it in the first place, yet in the process reveal too much about myself. It was a lose-lose situation. But if I didn't write about it now, I would never write about it, and thus, would forever curse my cowardice.

The door to my office opened, and a man about 40, wearing a dark-blue suit, a white button-down shirt, a wide blue-and-white striped tie, and spit-shiny black wingtips walked in. He stood about six feet tall, was solidly built with wide square shoulders and a narrow waist, was clean shaven, and had short dark hair, blue eyes, and tiny drops of melted snow on his shoes. Although I had never seen him before, I instinctively knew who he was and why he was there.

"Garth Ryland?" he said.

"Speaking."

"I'm special agent John Stevenson of the FBI." He showed me his identification, but didn't offer to shake my hand.

"Have a seat," I said.

"I won't be here that long."

"Then I hope you don't mind if I don't get up." I was

sitting in my swivel captain's chair. I had turned around to face him.

"Wherever's comfortable." He pocketed his wallet. "I'll cut right to the chase, Mr. Ryland, and save us both time. Why were you talking to Michelle Gustavson this afternoon?"

"We had a fire. She was an eyewitness. As a newspaperman, it just seemed reasonable to me."

"According to my sources, your questions were of an investigative nature."

"There is such a thing as investigative journalism. Surely even you in the FBI have heard of it."

"And what are you investigating? Not the fire, I hope."

I shrugged. "It's a free country. The last time I looked anyway."

"Maybe I will need that chair."

I gestured toward the east wall where the chairs stood. "Be my guest. Either one is guaranteed to give you numbbutt."

He carried the chair to within three feet of my desk and sat down with the back of the chair facing me and his legs astraddle the seat. He didn't appear to be a hard case, but you never knew. One didn't get to be a special agent of the FBI by taking a correspondence course.

"Let's start over," he said. "What did Miss Gustavson have to say about the fire?"

"She said she was opening her east window to let in some air because she likes to sleep in the cold, when she saw the fire in the church. Subsequently she saw, or thought she might have seen, she wasn't sure, someone leave the church and run in a northeasterly direction. Even though she wasn't completely sure she saw anyone at all, she was sure enough to identify him as a man rather than a woman."

He reached into his inside coat pocket for a small notebook. As he did, I noticed the strap of his shoulder holster.

"That's pretty sure, I'd say," he said, making a note of it. "Anything else?"

"That's it as far as the fire goes. We talked a little bit about her family, since I knew her father from when he used to preach in Madison."

"When was that?"

"The mid-60s. You probably were in grade school then."

He nodded, neither agreeing nor disagreeing. "Do you believe what Miss Gustavson told you?"

"Why? Don't you?"

"I asked first."

"I have my doubts. But don't quote me on that."

"So do I," he said.

"May I ask yours?"

"Nobody that pretty can ever be believed. That's my first rule of thumb."

"Sounds cynical to me. Or sexist."

"Or both." He stood and offered his hand, which I shook. "I hope I won't be seeing you again."

"In other words, butt out. Is that what you're saying?"

He carried the chair back to the wall and set it down

in the exact spot where he'd found it. Impressive, but of course he had its imprints in the dust to guide him.

"That's what I'm saying," he said. "We have our own method of doing things. You'll only be in the way."

"Perhaps. But don't forget. Oakalla is my town, not yours. And it will still be my town when you leave."

"So everyone here keeps reminding me." He went as far as the office door where he stopped. "By the way, have you seen Marshal Hardwick lately?"

"Not lately."

"I need to talk to him. You have any idea where he might be?"

"Home, most likely. Getting his beauty rest."

He shook his head as if clearing out the cobwebs, as if he couldn't quite comprehend it all. "Are all small towns like this one?"

"Most of them. Give or take a few idiosyncrasies. Or idiots. Take your choice."

He left, still shaking his head in disbelief. I leaned a little further back into my chair, wondering why Michelle had sicced him on me. I'd thought we'd parted friends.

The phone rang. "Garth. Cecil here. You talk to Michelle Gustavson yet?"

"About an hour ago."

"She tell you about the man she saw leaving the church?"

"Yes."

"What do you make of that?"

"I've been lied to by experts. I think she might be among the best."

"So left you feeling snookered, just like me."

"I didn't at the time, but I'm starting to. Not that it matters."

"Why wouldn't it?"

"Even as we speak, there's an FBI agent by the name of John Stevenson on his way to your house to tell you to leave the fire alone."

"Can he do that?"

"Yes. I believe there's a law on the books to that effect. So if you don't want to hear what he has to say, you'd better get out of the house before he can warn you off."

"Did you get the same message?"

"Yes."

"What are *you* going to do about it?"

"I'm going to put out a newspaper, then go looking for Camelia Capers. As for you, I'd stick with Plan B. It seems to me a good one."

"You mean lie low during the day and hit the streets at night."

"Yes. Nobody can fault you for that and who knows what you might see. Just be careful, that's all. We don't know everything we're dealing with here."

"You mean those bullet holes in that pickup weren't self-inflicted?"

"That's exactly what I mean."

"Have to go, Garth. Company's coming up the drive."

"Stay in touch."

"I'll be sure to."

CHAPTER 15

I could feel rather than see the snow as I walked to the Corner Bar and Grill for supper. Already it was night, and Oakalla had turned back the spread and put its boots in front of the stove, giving its empty streets the look and feel of desolation. Neither did it help my spirits any to know that there was a full moon up there somewhere, if I could just see it.

A few of the regulars were clustered around the bar, but except for Larry Don Loomus, who sat in the northwest corner booth drinking a Bud Light, the rest of the barroom was empty. Larry Don looked lonely sitting there in his Carharts and hiking boots, and angry about something. I decided to join him.

"You want company?" I said.

He continued to stare straight ahead, as if he hadn't heard.

I was spared having to ask again when Hiram hurried

over to take my order. He knew, as was the case every Thursday night, I would be in a hurry.

"How do *you* rate?" Larry Don said sullenly after Hiram left. "I damn near broke my arm flagging him down."

I took the seat across from him. "I live here, remember."

"Sorry. I keep forgetting that *I* am the pariah."

If I were to guess by the look and sound of him, that wasn't Larry Don's first Bud Light of the evening sitting there. He was measuring his words, which made his southern accent that much more pronounced, and out of place there in the frozen northland—a fact not likely lost on him.

"No use asking if you've found Camelia Capers yet," I said.

He shook his head no. "But since you have been so kind as to broach the subject, I have tried on several occasions to get through to Mr. Orion, but he isn't taking any calls, as I am told he is someplace other than Emerald City. So I am wondering how you, a stranger, could break through his long chain of command and reach him, when I, his own confederate, cannot?"

"I didn't reach him. Sheriff Stonewall Jackson Huff did."

"That fat old cracker. He wouldn't make the effort."

"It appears he did."

"Or told you he did. Just to get to me."

"I wasn't aware that you and he were more than passing acquaintances," I said.

"Who's that, sir?"

Larry Don finished the Bud Light and banged the empty bottle down on the table loudly enough for a couple of the regulars to turn around to see what the problem was. Hiram, however, ignored him.

"You walking or driving?" I said.

"Walking. Who can drive in this weather. Who in their right mind wants to."

I waved Hiram over and said, "We need another Bud Light, Hiram. It's on me."

"He walking or driving?"

"Walking."

"You know best, I suppose."

Actually I didn't know squat. I just wanted to keep Larry Don talking.

"You and Sheriff Huff," I said, picking up where we'd left off. "I thought you and he knew who each other by reputation, but that was about it."

"Maybe he wanted to give you that impression, but Sheriff Huff and I have dug in the same sweet potato patch several times before, and not always to his liking. The man is no bargain, sir. You have my word on that."

"Do you think he's in Orion's pocket?"

"I would not put it past him. No."

Hiram brought me my fish sandwich, onion rings, and Dr. Pepper, and Larry Don his Bud Light. A draft of Leinenkugels would have gone nicely with my fish sandwich, but I still had my column to write.

"Do you not drink?" Larry Don asked.

"I've got to put out my newspaper tonight. I'll need a clear head for that."

"Discipline. I like that in a man. You can always trust him to hold his block."

"It's my understanding that Orion is very disciplined," I said.

Larry Don rose unsteadily on his bum leg and said, "Exceptions to every rule, my friend. Exceptions to every rule."

He limped noticeably as he made his way through the swinging door and out the barroom. For the second time since we had met, he had left a gift of mine untouched. I was starting to think he didn't like me.

I had no more returned to my office when Clarkie called. He said, "I'm just touching base to let you know where I am in this, which isn't very far I'm afraid. There's nothing in our data bank, or any of those I've accessed, that has anything on Orion. He has no criminal record, no outstanding warrants, not even a parking ticket that I can find. So I'm at a dead end there, unless I can think of something else."

It was disappointing news, but not unexpected. "Don't worry about it, Clarkie. There's something else I'd like for you to do for me, if you would. I'd like to know of any and all church fires in south-central Wisconsin in say the past couple years. But don't let anyone know you're doing it, or we'll both be in trouble."

"Who with?"

"The FBI. I've already been warned off once."

"That information is public knowledge. I don't see why that would be a problem to them. Unless they know something that you don't."

"I think that's the case. Which is why I'm asking for help."

"Okay. I'll find some way around it. What else?"

"That's it. Unless you can find a way to come up with Orion's true identity."

"Give me another shot at it. How soon do you need to know about the churches?"

"As soon as possible. We lost ours yesterday."

"I'm sorry, Garth. Aunt Norma told me about it."

"Did we make the *Capital Times*?"

"It and Channel 15 both."

"I figured we might."

"Is there something you know that you aren't telling anybody?"

"Just a hunch, Clarkie. It probably won't lead anywhere."

"I'll bet," he said with misplaced confidence.

"Remember what I said. Mum's the word."

"You can trust me, Garth."

And so I could.

Four hours, and a half dozen cups of instant coffee later, I finally finished my column and called in my printer before I changed my mind. Then I walked to the north window of my office to see if Oakalla had disappeared in my absence and was heartened to learn that it hadn't. Although shrouded by a spittle of snow, its street lights continued to burn, its chimneys continued to smoke, and its houses continued to stand fast against the cold.

Serenity as I knew it depended on that assurance— the faith that while your back was turned someone would not steal your life, your family, your home, your church; the faith that what you so loved today would not be arbitrarily taken from you tomorrow. Of course, there were no guarantees. The very beauty of life was its transience, its frailty, its utter contempt for plans and permanence. We hoped that God would keep us and those we loved safe from harm, but could not be absolutely sure since, the fallen sparrow not withstanding, bad things *did* happen to good people, which left us wanting in the way of assurance.

Some had their rituals and their dogmas, which they would wear like a suit of armor to the grave, and beyond, if necessary. Others had their living faith, which hoped all good things for themselves and others, transcended all tragedies, and made their lives a witness for the poor in spirit. Others had no patience either for religion or those who practiced it, and found their salvation either in science, nature, the arts, or themselves.

But for those of us who once walked in faith and now found ourselves outside of it, wanting to believe in God's infinite goodness, yet as a witness to history, unable to, only the church of our childhood remained. We could no longer find salvation there. Yet the solitude within its brick walls was strangely comforting, its hard oak pews gentle to our weary bodies, its coolness refreshing on a hot summer afternoon. We did not stop by there often, but often enough to remind ourselves of all that had been lost, all that had been gained in "living every day." And sometimes on our Sunday morning walks we would stop to hear the old upright Sunday school piano, and the songs flung out the chapel windows by the kids we once were—songs we knew by heart, songs that went straight to our soul.

Never mind that my great-grandfather Ruff had helped found the church, that my parents and their parents were married there, that it was the site of my baptism and my grandmother's funeral. When you burned down my church, you burned more than my history. You burned my sanctuary, the one place in Oakalla where I could go and be absolutely free from the cares of the world.

Why did you do it? I wished I knew. I hoped it wasn't a random act of vandalism, done on a dare or a whim, or a drunken rampage. I hoped it wasn't to hide, or disguise another crime; or some petty grievance against one of the church members or religion itself.

No, I would rather the church had done you a grievous wrong, failed you somehow in your desperate hour of need, and left you still immersed in your unending hell. I'd rather you had begged for its tender mercies and instead received a crown of thorns, had your honor or your innocence or the whole of your being damned by its indifference to your pain, or its cowardice in the face of evil.

Vengeance, I could understand. Vengeance, I might overlook—had you chosen someone else's church to burn.

"Well?" I said after my printer had read my column.

In our weekly ritual, I proofed the first paper off the press for typos while he proofed my column for content. Though we neither one much liked criticism, neither was shy about speaking his mind.

"It'll fly," he said.

Good enough for me.

Once we had put all the mailing labels on the papers, we bundled them and put them in the back of my printer's old green Pontiac station wagon for their ride to the post office. He took it from there.

Too wired from all of the coffee I'd drunk to go home, I decided to pay Beezer's place another visit to see if anything had changed there. The walk was not unpleasant, but dark once I left the street lights behind. And cold, even though the wind was at my back.

Beezer's place felt the same as it had the other times I was there, neither warmer nor colder, which in itself bothered me. I wished I'd thought to bring a thermometer to see if it really was warmer in there than it should have been, or if I was too acclimated to the cold outside to tell.

As before, Beezer's stove didn't feel cold to touch, but then neither did it feel warm, and when I used his poker to stir the ashes, I found no live coals. The rest of the place, seen in the glare of Beezer's hanging light, showed no change. Perhaps I was indulging myself, making a place seem inhabited that was not.

I went back outside, and when I reached Gas Line Road, was startled to find another set of fresh footprints there besides my own. They stopped where I had turned into Beezer's, and then they headed back toward town.

As I followed them, then lost them in a set of tire tracks at the junction of Park Street and Gas Line Road, I knew that I had followed them before. Except this time the hare had turned hound before turning back to hare again. I didn't like the thought. Someone was on to me and didn't care if I knew it.

CHAPTER 16

I awakened to the smell of coffee perking and bacon frying and thanked God for Saturdays—until I realized that it wasn't Saturday, but Friday instead. Ruth should have been at the shelter by then. Why wasn't she?

"What's the occasion?" I said.

"No occasion," Ruth said. "I figured you could use a good breakfast for once."

"Who's minding the store?"

"I am. Once I leave here."

Maybe I'd figure it out later. "You read my column yet?"

"Yes."

"And?"

"It needed to be said." High praise from her.

"Thank you."

"But don't expect everyone who reads it to agree."

"I can live with that." I walked over to the stove to pour us each a cup of coffee.

She had six strips of bacon frying in a cast iron skillet. She used two forks to individually turn each piece when it had cooked on one side. Meanwhile I stirred a spoonful of sugar and a splash of half-and-half into each of our cups, then set Ruth's cup on the counter beside her.

"You came in later than usual last night," she said.

After I put the *Reporter* to bed, I took a walk out to Beezer's to see if he'd come back yet. He hadn't. But someone followed me out there. I spent another hour or so trying to find out whom."

"How do you know someone followed you out there?"

"I saw his tracks in the snow. They went as far as Beezer's, then turned around and came back into town."

"How do you know it was a man?"

"By the size of the tracks."

She took a drink of coffee as she thought about it. "Why would he want to follow you out to Beezer's?"

"Maybe he thinks I know something he doesn't."

"Which is?"

"Where Camelia Capers is hiding."

"Do you?"

"No." That seemed to come as a relief to her, but I didn't ask why.

"Do you have any idea who the man was who followed you?" she asked.

"Larry Don would be my guess. I doubt it was the first time either. He seems to know his way around Oakalla pretty well by now."

"Well enough to start a fire right next to the shelter to flush Camelia out of hiding?"

"No. Larry Don would have set fire to the shelter, not the church across the street, if he thought she were inside."

"And burn up all that money he's supposedly chasing?"

She had me there. "What about William Gustavson? You learn anything about him?" I said.

She could smirk without appearing to, just to let me know that she'd won the round. "I learned that you were right. He did kill a man early on in his ministry. He was riding shotgun with a state trooper friend of his down around Janesville when the trooper pulled a man over for a routine traffic stop. Before anyone could stop him, the man jumped out of his car and started shooting. Though fatally wounded, the trooper still managed to return fire long enough for William Gustavson to take the trooper's shotgun from its rack and open fire on the man who'd shot his friend. He killed the man, and in the process ruined his career. He was a terrific speaker and leader from what I understand and had bishop written all over him. But even though he preached in some of the biggest churches around, including those in Madison, he never even made district superintendent, let alone bishop. And even those plum churches started going to other younger ministers after a few years."

"All because he killed a man in self-defense?"

She rose to finish cooking breakfast. Unless she were reading or watching a Packers game, she couldn't stay seated for long.

"From my understanding of the Methodist Discipline, an eye for an eye is not part of the job description. It might work in politics, Garth, but not in the ministry."

"Still, it's a harsh judgment against him. He was the best, Ruth, the absolute best I ever heard."

"So you've told me." She was less sympathetic than I, but unlike me, she'd never had to kill anyone.

"Where is William Gustavson now?"

"Florida, I think."

"That's what Janie said."

"It's Janie now, is it?"

"Relax, Ruth. If I'd said Reverend Gustavson, you wouldn't know which one I was talking about."

"I thought you didn't like her sermons."

"I don't. But I like her. As a person, that's all," I said to ward off any further comment on the subject. "I'm not as sure about her daughter."

"What's wrong with her?"

"Besides the fact I think she's a liar, she sicced the FBI on me."

"Maybe you deserved it."

"I didn't think so. But maybe she did."

"Why do you think she's a liar?"

I finally told her.

"You might have a point."

"Sometimes I do."

Ruth was in the process of mixing pancake batter. "So where are you off to today?"

"Fickle Store."

"What's left there to find?"

"Answers, I hope."

On my way out to the garage I let Daisy into the house so that she could keep Ruth company until Ruth left for the shelter. Ruth, however, who was still washing breakfast dishes, seemed in no hurry to get to the shelter that morning, which made me wonder what she was up to.

Jessie, the brown Chevy sedan that I had inherited from Grandmother Ryland, had a long sorry history of failing me at critical moments. I had been urged by many in Oakalla, Ruth in particular, to get another car, one that I not only could depend on, but drive in some comfort. With Jessie, I never knew from one day to the next when I might lose heat, fan, radio, windshield wipers, and other such things that most people took for granted.

But I had resisted all calls to replace Jessie and my own murderous impulses to drive her over the nearest cliff. She ran. Not well, willingly, with either style or grace, but she ran. Until she glugged her last hit of gas and gave up the ghost, I was stuck with her—out of loyalty, if nothing else.

The day seemed unchanged from the previous ones. It was still cloudy, cold, and somber, with the threat of snow in the air. The only difference was that it wasn't snowing. Yet. I was certain that it would be before day's end.

Jessie's best speed was 45, downhill, with a tail wind, so she balked a little on the flats between Oakalla and Fickle when I tried to goose her up to 50. Otherwise, our trip to Fickle was uneventful, which is to say we made it.

Jasper Peterson was outside with a hoe digging through the ruins of his store. The rubble by then had stopped smoking and was covered with a blanket of snow, which had reduced it to a large white lump in an otherwise uniform landscape. Had Jasper not been so intent on exposing its black underbelly, no one would ever have known that there had been a fire there—let alone a store where thousands of stories had been swapped and thousands of dollars had changed hands.

"Finding anything worth keeping?" I said.

Jasper wore the same brown slacks that I had seen him in last, the same blue hooded sweatshirt, the same caterpillar mustache, the same blank lost look on his face, as if, since he really didn't know where to go from here, this was the best he could do.

"No. To tell the truth, I'm just killing time," he said. "Waiting for the insurance company to clear me so that I can collect the money on the store."

"The FBI been by?"

"Yesterday. They didn't stay long." Jasper's smile had a bitter slant to it. "They had bigger fish to fry."

"They give you a hard time?"

"Not as hard of time as the insurance company's been

giving me. I hated to hear about the church burning down, but I was glad it took some of the heat off of me." Again his smile had a bitter edge.

"How so?" I said.

"Well, from the get go the insurance company had me pegged for the fire here at the store, seeing there was no one else around at the time and nobody I could identify as a possible suspect. So just because my revenues have been down the last couple years and look to go down even more once Carl Bolin has his store there at the crossroads up and running, my natural next step, according to the insurance company, was to burn my store down and, once I get their money, light out for the territories."

"It's not a bad plan," I said.

Jasper leaned on his hoe as he looked me straight in the eye. "Except it didn't happen that way."

"Why are revenues down?" I said, as he began raking away the snow to get to the rubble below. "Don't people drink as much beer as they used to?"

He stopped hoeing and again aimed his one good eye at me. "That's only a small part of my trade, Garth. And to lay another matter to rest, I didn't know that Marshal Hardwick's nephew was underage when he bought the beer. His ID said he was of age, so what was I to do? Hell, probably half the kids I sell to are underage, but if they've got identification that says otherwise, that's good enough for me. Let their parents look after them. It's not my job."

He went back to hoeing up Campbell soup cans with me watching him.

"But to answer your question, Garth, what I don't sell as much of as I used to is live bait. People, young people in particular, don't seem to fish as much as they used to. They'd rather party, or play their video games, or ride their jet skis to hell and back. And those that in years past might have been fishermen take up sailing or canoeing instead. Not that it's a dying art, but one of these days, when all of us old-timers are gone, it might be."

"Maybe it's all for the good. The fish around here probably could use a rest."

"But bad for the people who make it their stock and trade."

I thought I felt a snowflake bite my cheek, but it could have been one of those that Jasper was stirring up.

"Two years ago when the cabin over on Coon Lake burned down, do you remember anything else out of the ordinary that night?" I said.

"Nope. Except that I could have sworn I shut those gas pumps off before I left the store that evening. I automatically do it every night. Why not that night?"

"Perhaps someone came in and turned them on."

"How? The place was all locked up."

"The same way they got in Monday night."

"You mean down the coal chute?"

"It's a possibility."

Jasper had his doubts. "They'd almost have to know the store by heart to have done that."

"Off the record, does anyone come to mind?"

"Outside of Carl Bolin, no."

"Why Carl Bolin?"

"His mother sold the store to me out from under him. But I bet you already knew that."

"What I meant was that this isn't the same store that the Friedricksons owned."

"No. But after he got out of the service, Carl worked for me for a while. Long enough for him to realize that he didn't really want to be a storekeeper after all."

"Then why is he planning on starting one?"

"That seems pretty obvious. To run me out of business."

"Maybe I should hear his side of it."

He shrugged. "Fair's fair."

On my way to White Lick, I took a detour at Coon Lake to see what I might see. I got out of Jessie at the site of the former cabin and walked toward shore, where I discovered fresh footprints in the snow. They led to the edge of the water, then along the shore, until they turned around about 200 yards to the north and returned the way they'd come.

Facing the lake, gray and sullen with a slight chop softly plopping against the shore, I could feel sand-like flakes of snow burn my cheek. Someone, a woman by all appearances, had parked her car and taken a walk right across the site where the cabin used to sit, then turned and gone about an eighth of a mile along the lake. Neither was it the first time that she had done so. What was the attraction, I wondered? And why did I feel that this was a dark ritual, rather than a light-hearted romp in the snow?

White Lick is one of those towns that make you wonder how they came to be in the first place, and why they are still there. Built along County Road J two miles after it crossed State Road 13, White Lick had no railroad running through it, no river, or major highway, or anything else that said a town should be there. The Wisconsin River was a few miles to the west, but County Road J turned north at the river, so there was no way to cross the river, even if there was someplace on the other side that you wanted to go.

Not that White Lick was much of a town. It had at most a hundred residents, most of them over 50, and all of its houses, with their log bottoms and steeply slanted brown roofs, had seen more than their share of Wisconsin winters and had the scars to prove it.

But it did have a couple antique shops, a couple taverns, a post office, general store, and Catholic Church, and Carl Bolin's real estate office, where I found him on the phone trying to cut a deal with someone who apparently had some wrought iron fence for sale.

"Be with you in a minute," he said to me as he covered the mouthpiece.

"I'm in no hurry."

Carl Bolin was a burly man of about 40, with curly

blond hair, thick bushy sideburns, Viking blue eyes, and the ruddy sandpaper complexion of someone who spent a lot of the year out of doors. His real estate office was in the front part of a long low log building that looked as if it might have been used for boat storage in the past, or to house the Ringling Brothers whenever they came to town. His office walls were log, as was the counter that separated his desk and filing cabinets from the rest of the office. A muskey was mounted on the east wall, along with a walleye and a lake trout. The muskey looked to be about 30 pounds, the lake trout about the same, and the walleye seven or eight pounds. The only thing I knew for certain, outside of the fact that they were all dead, was that none of them had come out of Coon Lake in the past 15 years. Otherwise, I would have heard about it.

"You in the antique business, too?" I said after he was off the phone.

He pointed east, the direction from which I'd come. "You see those two antique shops on your way into town? They're both mine."

"Why two?"

"It's simple. People come in here looking for bargains. They figure what could country hicks like us know about antiques? As if we couldn't read the same books they do. So I try to give them what they want. Price the hell out of some things in the one store. Have the same thing dirt cheap in the other." He winked at me. "Or so it seems."

"Sounds like you've got all the bases covered," I said.

"I found out the hard way it doesn't hurt."

"By the way, I'm Garth Ryland," I said, offering my hand.

"I know. I recognized you from your picture in the paper."

He had a grip that could crack a walnut. I was grateful when he finally let go.

"And your name?" I said, feigning ignorance.

"I figure you know that already, which is why you're here."

"You don't miss much, do you?"

"Like I said a minute ago, I learned my lessons the hard way."

"Does that include Fickle Store?"

He smiled, craned his neck to see beyond me outside. "It's snowing again, isn't it?" he said.

"Trying to."

"Looks like a long winter ahead."

"I've never known a short one yet. Not in Wisconsin anyway."

"You lived here long?"

"The past 30 years or so."

"So you're not a native."

"No. But I feel like one."

He leaned against the counter, resting on his forearms, which looked as hard and rippled as iron wood. "You been talking to Jasper Peterson?" he said.

"I just came from there."

"I suppose he's blaming me for the fire. But if you want my two cents worth, Jasper started the fire himself."

"You have proof of that?"

He shook his head no. "Wish I did, though. Nothing would give me greater pleasure than to deliver Jasper Peterson's head to you on a platter."

"Because your mother sold Fickle Store to him?"

"That's part of it. I was overseas in the service with no vote in the matter, and no way home, even if I'd had a vote. But I didn't mind him buying the store as much as I did him burning it down a few months later."

"You're sure about that?"

"I wasn't until this week. Two fires in 20 years, both to his advantage?"

I thought it over and decided that it could go either way. While true that both fires seemed to benefit Jasper, in the last fire at least, there appeared to be other candidates besides Jasper for setting the fire.

"Then why did you go to work for him if you knew what he'd done?" I said.

"I needed a job. When I got out of the service, times were tough. I figured his money would spend as well as anybody else's."

"No other reason for taking that job?"

Carl Bolin's hard-edged smile had no give to it. "I wanted to see how he operated. See if I could catch him at something. But I never did. Give the man credit, he's one slick operator."

"Maybe he's a shrewd but honest man who knows how to run a business."

"Tell that to the parents of the kid who died after drinking his booze."

"Jasper said the kid had an ID."

"That's what I would expect him to say."

"You'll never make a case against him," I said. "With that or the fire. You'll have to be satisfied with running him out of business."

Carl Bolin seemed to take no pleasure in the thought. "Big whoop. For 20 years I've been thinking how I could get even with the man and now, when everything's in place, I'll be denied the satisfaction. Jasper will take the insurance money and run. You just wait and see."

"Plus there's that lake property you're about to lose money on," I said.

"Who told you about that?"

"It's a small world. Word travels fast."

"Well, this is one case where I don't care if I do lose money. That place is haunted."

He appeared to be serious. At least he didn't wink at me.

"You've seen the ghost?"

"Yes. It started a year ago last summer. I kept getting all these complaints from the neighbors about this ghost walking their shoreline late at night, as if it was somehow my fault, just because I owned the property where she used to live. So I decided to put a stop to it once and for all. Sure enough, about a week after I started staking out the place, here she comes along the shore. Hey! I shouted, running toward her." Carl Bolin's eyes had started to water and I could see the hair rise on his forearms. "Then the damndest thing happened. She disappeared. . ." He snapped his fingers. It sounded like a rifle shot. "Just like that."

"Into the water?"

"How in the hell do I know? I assume that's where she went."

"And you never saw her again that night?"

"No. I didn't go looking either."

"What did she look like?"

"What do you mean, what did she look like? A damn ghost, that's what she looked like. Long dark hair, a long white dress, an easy way of walking that made her seem to just glide along. I'm not a believer either, Ryland. But she could make me one."

"Did you ever see her again after that night?"

"Only her tracks in the snow the other day."

"What day was that?"

"The day after Fickle Store burned."

"Why were you there then?"

"I thought I might have a buyer for the place. But he never showed up."

"Ghosts don't leave footprints, you know," I said.

"This one does. So if you're looking for some lake property, I'll make you one heck of a deal."

"I'll make a note of it."

"And Ryland," he said as I made my way to the door, "You see Jasper Peterson again, tell him if he'll stay, I'll help him rebuild."

"Why would you do that?"

He smiled. I imagined it was the same smile that Eric the Red wore as he raised his battle-ax. "So I'll have the pleasure of plowing him under."

CHAPTER 17

Back in Oakalla, I stopped at the intersection of Madison Road and Fickle Road, wondering where to go next, when I saw Janie Gustavson walk out the front door of the church carrying what appeared to be a candelabrum and a black book of some kind. I drove over there, parked alongside the sidewalk, and waited for her.

Deep in thought, she had already passed by me when I rolled down the window and said, "Need a ride?"

I startled her. As she spun around to face me, she nearly dropped the candelabrum and had to double-clutch to gain control of it again.

"How long have you been sitting there?" she said as she approached Jessie.

"About five seconds. Why?"

She shook her head wearily. "I must be losing my mind."

Janie wore jeans and a jean jacket and a black smudge

on her cheek. Her smile was bright, but her face was pale, and her eyes had a haunted cast to them, as if she had just encountered a ghost of her own.

"Where's all your help?" I said, reaching through the window and taking the candelabrum from her.

"I sent them home. No one is supposed to be in the church, including me, until after the investigation is over. But as you can see, I'm having a hard time staying away."

"What's that?" I said, referring to the charred black book that she carried.

"A Bible. King James version. I found it along with a bunch of old hymnals stuffed in the back of a closet."

It looked too thin to be a King James version, so it must have been a pocket edition.

"Hop in," I said.

"Why don't you hop out? I need the exercise."

Sure. Just like Seattle needed more rain. But I got out and joined her on the sidewalk.

"I read your column today. You missed your calling," she said, as we started walking toward the parsonage.

"Right. I should've been a preacher. Ruth tells me that every time I climb on my soapbox."

She took my arm, leaning against me as we walked. Taken or not, I could grow to like having her there.

"I was about to say, you should have been a poet. You have a poet's way with words."

"But, thank God, not a poet's income."

"Money isn't everything."

"No. But as a fellow cynic once so aptly put it, 'It sure beats whatever's in second place.'"

"You're not a cynic. You can't be and still care about things as much as you do." She leaned away from me so that she could look into my face. "God included."

"I care about God. I'm not so sure He cares about me."

"As much as He does anyone else. I even bet you're one of His favorites."

"The prodigal son."

She smiled then leaned into me again. "Could be."

We climbed the steps of the parsonage. I noticed that the snow, while still barely visible, had left a dusting there.

"Would you like to come in?" she said at the front door. "I'm sure I can find something for lunch."

"Best offer I've had all day."

I followed her all the way through the parsonage to the kitchen, which occupied the south end of the bottom floor of the house. Unlike the dark bricks outside, the kitchen had an open airy look and feel, a high white ceiling, a large window on the east side, a large window on the west side, and a window on each side of the back door. It also had white cabinets with black knobs, a white wooden table with square legs and four white wooden chairs around it, black linoleum with white swirls, and two black-and-red throw rugs, one in front of the sink and the other in front of the back door.

I set the candelabrum down and washed my hands in

the kitchen sink. Castile soap. I hadn't used it since I was a kid in Godfrey, Indiana.

Janie meanwhile had excused herself and gone upstairs. When she came back down again, her jean jacket was gone, along with the charred Bible and the black smudge on her cheek. Her light brown sweater, which had the softness of cashmere, was a perfect match for her hair.

"Why didn't you tell me I had a dirty face?" she said in mild reproach.

"It didn't bother me."

"Then you're forgiven, I guess. How does tomato soup and grilled cheese sandwiches sound?"

"Like a winner."

"Are you always so agreeable?"

"Usually," I said, and we let it go at that.

As she stood on her tiptoes, digging around in the cabinet while (I assumed) looking for the tomato soup, I found myself admiring her in ways that had escaped me before. Her legs were the slender, strong pins of a Thoroughbred, and had the taut trim line of a longbow. Dressed in her ministerial robe, she had appeared almost flat, to have no hips or breasts at all. Now that I could see what the robe had been hiding, I wished that I had taken another way home.

"You need any help?" I said.

"If you don't mind. I know it's in there someplace, but I can't find it."

She stepped aside as I scanned the top shelf of the cabinet. It was a reach even for me, but I finally dug a can of tomato soup out from behind a can of pork-and-beans and two cans of crushed pineapple. The can looked dusty enough to have come with the parsonage.

"You must not eat soup often," I said, handing the can to her.

"No. Not very."

I couldn't wait to see the cheese. "You done with me?"

Her smile warmed me in places it shouldn't. "For now."

I sat back down at the table and prayed for divine intervention. "Something about the fire that I forgot to ask you and should have," I said.

It grew noticeably still in there. "Yes?"

"Do you keep the church locked?"

"Everything but the front door."

"Why leave it open?"

"Because there has to be some way in. Somebody might need in there to pray."

"Or to rest his weary soul," I said.

"Yes. That too. But I've had a real hassle with the official board about it. They're afraid someone might come in there . . . Well, you know. Burn down the place."

The sparkle had left her eyes. They were as milky as jade.

"You can't blame yourself for that," I said.

"No. But I do."

The phone rang. It was only two steps away, but Janie made no move to answer it.

"We have an answering machine in the living room," she said. "I don't feel like talking to anyone right now."

But when Janie's recorded voice in the person of

Reverend Gustavson answered, the caller hung up. Janie took that as her cue to continue with lunch.

As she beat a path between the stove and the refrigerator, I noted that, unlike Ruth and Abby, she didn't seem to know her way around her own kitchen very well. I wondered what she and Michelle did for their meals and imagined that they ate a lot of frozen dinners, because there were no fast food restaurants in Oakalla, and she'd had to ask for help with the menu at the Corner Bar and Grill, which meant that it wasn't a regular stop. So that made this, her effort on my behalf, even more special, and me even more appreciative.

"I'm sorry it's taking so long," she said, as she searched the refrigerator for something. "As you can tell, I'm a little rusty at this."

"Don't be sorry. I'm enjoying your company."

"There's a can of mixed nuts in the cabinet beside the stove."

"I'll be fine."

The back door banged open and Michelle Gustavson rushed in with the same angry look on her face I'd seen the night of the fire. "Oh! It's you again," she said on seeing me. "I might have known."

"You're just in time for lunch," Janie said calmly. "If you'll tell me where you put the cheese."

"Mom, I have to talk to you," Michelle said.

"So talk."

Michelle glanced from her mother to me, not sparing either of us her anger. "In private."

"Can't it wait until this evening?"

"No. It can't wait. I'm cutting class as it is."

Janie let her hand trail across my shoulders on her way out of the kitchen. "I'll be right back," she said.

Then Janie and Michelle went upstairs to talk. Although I couldn't hear what they were saying, I could tell by Michelle's heated outbursts that she was the one on the offensive. Janie, on the other hand, never raised her voice, or if she did, I didn't hear her.

A few minutes later Janie came into the kitchen looking worn out and beaten down—so far down that she seemed beyond tears. "I'm sorry, Garth. This is more serious than I thought. Perhaps you'd like to take a rain check?"

"Sure."

As I got up from the table, I took her in my arms and held her. At first she stiffened in resistance, then relaxed and let go. I had never known anyone who needed a cry more.

"Mom? Mom?" Michelle yelled down the stairs.

"God, when am I ever going to have a life of my own?" Janie said as she pulled away and went back upstairs.

I let myself out. As I made my way to Jessie, I realized that divine intervention had occurred, that for the first time in a long time I had visible proof that a prayer of mine had been answered. Which told me: (1) God had not lost His sense of humor, and (2) in the future I might be a little more careful about what I prayed for.

CHAPTER 18

I had that long awaited draft of Leinenkugels with my lunch at the Corner Bar and Grill, then spent the rest of the afternoon until dark in my office not answering the phone. My desk was solid oak, three feet wide and five feet long, and had come from the boiler room of my father's dairy. So had the captain's chair in which I sat as I rested my feet on my desk. I always retreated to them whenever I felt vulnerable or out of sorts or I had thinking to do, as was the case today. But try though I might, I couldn't make all of the pieces of the past few days fit the same puzzle. And with so many wildcards still in the deck, I feared that the worst might be yet to come.

With a sigh of relief I parked Jessie in the garage and shut off her engine. We had gone to Fickle and back, to my office and then home without a hitch. It was almost enough to make me shout hallelujah! The drought is broken. But I knew better.

The snow had been with us for so many days now that I almost didn't notice its peck, peck, peck against my cheek on my way to the house. Daisy, her hackles raised, stood with her front paws against the south fence barking at something. Although never trained as a watchdog, she did have a good nose for trouble, so whenever she barked, which was seldom, I paid attention.

"What is it, girl?" I said, going to her.

Her answer was to bark louder, even more fiercely.

I could have opened the gate and let her out, which would have solved one problem, but created a second. When freed, Daisy went hunting. Unless she found something to point, and in this case I couldn't be sure that she would, she would keep going until she did. Not wanting to spend the night in Illinois, I took her inside before the neighbors started calling.

"What's wrong with Daisy?" Ruth said from the dining room.

"I wish I knew."

Daisy had run to the front door and stood there barking. She wasn't allowed past the kitchen, so she must have had her reasons.

I went after Daisy and saw that Ruth was sitting on the floor of the dining room with the bottom doors of the buffet open and a pile of stuff on the floor beside her. "What are you doing down there?" I said.

"Looking for something." She waved me away. "Go mind your own business."

I grabbed Daisy by her collar and led her to the basement, where she eagerly raced down the steps. A few seconds later I heard her barking again.

"What goes on here while I'm away?" I said to no one in particular.

"What's that?" Ruth said.

"Nothing. You planning on fixing supper or should I head on up to the Corner?"

"You'd better call Clarkie before you do anything else."

I walked out onto our front porch to see if I could see or hear whatever it was that had Daisy upset. The night, however, was impenetrable. It reminded me of the poem, "Ashes", I had written on the eve of my divorce, and the lines, "outside snow fell, dimming the dark with a thin mask of white."

"Why? Did Clarkie call here?" I said when back inside.

"No. He called me twice at the shelter. Weren't you in your office this afternoon?"

I felt lucky that I could tell her the truth, since I could just as easily have been in Janie Gustavson's bed. "Yes. I was in my office. But I wasn't answering the phone."

"Why not?"

"I was trying to put this week's events all in the same box. I can't."

"I can't either, if that helps any."

"It helps a lot, Ruth."

I called Clarkie. He answered after the first ring, so he must have been at his computer.

"Clarkie, it's Garth. Ruth said you've been trying to get hold of me."

"Yeah, I took the day off so that I could work on this. It was a slow day in the office, so the captain didn't mind. I've got a slew of them coming anyway."

"I appreciate it, Clarkie. But I don't want you to lose points on my account."

"That's not a problem, Garth. They need me here."

He left the rest of it unsaid. We in Oakalla had never felt that way about him.

"So what do you have for me?" I said.

"First things first, I guess. You have a pencil and paper handy?"

I grabbed the first pen that I could find then rummaged through that day's junk mail until I found a suitable envelope. "I do now."

"You wanted a list of the churches that had burned in the Madison area lately. They are the Olarno United Methodist Church, the Wheatville United Methodist Church, the Lake Ridge Catholic Church, the Boynette Community Church, and the Immanuel Lutheran Church just south of the Dells. There are others, but these are the only ones whose fires are of suspicious origin."

I hurriedly wrote all of them down, but then couldn't remember why I'd asked for them in the first place. Grasping at straws, I guessed. Since the FBI had warned me off, I wanted to see the cards they weren't showing.

"I hope you didn't use your computer on this," I said.

"No. I did it the old-fashioned way. Legwork. I went to the *Capital Times* and they let me go through their morgue."

"Are there any you could have missed?"

"Yes. But it's not likely."

"Sure of yourself, aren't you?" I said, enjoying his new-found confidence.

"I'm learning to be."

"You come across anything about Orion while you were there?"

"No. I had to use my computer for that. But you'll be glad to know I didn't hack."

"I'm proud of you, Clarkie," I said, not caring one way or another. As a computer novice, I had no feel for the ethics involved. You fed the beast and tried to keep it happy so that in turn it didn't devour you. That summed up my computer philosophy in a nutshell.

Then, since I knew that Clarkie was expecting me to, I said, "How did you manage that?"

"Went on the internet. I posted my want ad on bulletin boards all around the country, then sat back and waited. You'll never guess where the information came from."

I waited for him to tell me.

"Oakalla, Wisconsin."

"Shit," I said.

Ruth stopped her search long enough to give me the evil eye. She rarely swore and didn't approve of my doing it.

"What do you think about them apples?" Clarkie said.

"I'm thoughtless. You sure the information came from Oakalla?"

"That's what the e-mail message said. It was signed C.C., Oakalla, Wisconsin."

Camelia Capers, I bet.

"She give you a street address, Clarkie?"

"What do you want for nothing?"

"Sorry, I got greedy. What's her take on Orion?"

"Her words or mine?"

"Whichever." No matter what the subject, I almost always lost patience with Clarkie at some point in our dialogue.

"To start with, Orion's real name is Joe Dan Kidwell. He played split-end for the University of Southern Mississippi about ten years back, where he was known, among other things, for dealing drugs, though no arrests were ever made. He tried out for both the then Houston Oilers and the New Orleans Saints, but was cut by both teams. He dropped out of sight for a few years then reappeared as Orion of Emerald City, Mississippi." There Clarkie paused and began to read the e-mail message word for word. "Though he now claims to follow the straight and narrow, his past track record makes him out a liar. A leopard, after all, can't change its spots. How well I know."

"That's all?" I said, disappointed.

"How much do you want? I can't give you any more than what's there, Garth."

189

"Have you tried to reach C. C. again?"

"Yes. Several times. No one's answering."

"It really would help to know where C. C. is in Oakalla."

"Someplace where there's a computer. That's all I know."

"Thanks, Clarkie. At least I know she's still in town."

"I've got something else on Orion, if you're interested?"

"I'm interested."

"You wanted to know where the money that Camelia's mother has been sending to Orion has been going. Well, I got to thinking. What if he really is on the level about Camelia leaving, yet for some reason can't tell her mother that she's left. How could he take her money and still cover his tail? A trust fund in Camelia's name is what I came up with. So I nosed around until I found the right bank, then called, saying that because of the hurricane, I wasn't sure my last transaction had made it through, and had they received my check on Camelia Capers' account as scheduled." He paused. I could almost hear the drum roll. "They had."

"Clarkie, you're a genius."

"Pretty smart anyway. At times."

I wished that we were talking face to face. It would be fun to see him in one of his finer moments after all of the lesser moments behind us.

"As always, I owe you, Clarkie."

"And one of these days you'll pay up."

"So?" Ruth said after I'd hung up.

"Orion is the same enigma as always. That's the good news. The bad news is that Camelia is still here in Oakalla."

"Why isn't that good news?"

"Because I don't know where she is, and I don't want to have to go door to door looking for her."

"Maybe I can help."

I joined her at the dining room table where she had laid out the *1958 Oakalla Centennial Souvenir Booklet.* "I've been looking all over the house for this," she said. "It came to me, while walking home from the shelter this evening, where it might be." She pointed to a photograph of a beautiful dark-haired, dark-skinned young woman in a flapper outfit from the 1920s. "Recognize her?"

I recognized her immediately. "That's Camelia Capers." However, the caption read, "Harriet Jones."

"Who's Harriet Jones?" I said.

"Hattie Peeler. Jones was her maiden name."

"What kind of name is that for a Chippewa?"

"Hattie was adopted. That's why there's only one of her here."

I studied Hattie's photograph, and wished that she and I had been of the same generation. If not lovers, we could have been great friends.

"When did you put Hattie and Camelia together?" I said.

"Not until this morning. I woke up thinking about it then couldn't get it off my mind. You're the one who got the ball rolling, though, when you said that Camelia

191

looked familiar to you. She did to me as well, though for the life of me, I couldn't figure out why."

"Obviously she's not Hattie's daughter," I said.

Ruth took the booklet from me and made her own study of Hattie. Hattie's eyes in particular were worth noting. Bold, dark, arresting, with just a hint of arrogance, they spoke volumes about being the only Indian in town. Of course, now she was the only Native American.

"Grandmother would be my guess," Ruth said as she closed the booklet. "Hattie had a daughter late in life who left town at the first opportunity. The last I heard, she'd married a college professor down South somewhere."

"Hattiesburg, Mississippi would be my guess."

I rose and went to the hall closet to get my coat and stocking cap. The thought of going out into the cold again did nothing for my morale.

"Answer me one question, will you, Ruth? What is Hattie doing with a computer? She doesn't even own a television."

"You might ask her when you get there."

CHAPTER 19

Sometimes you don't think. Sometimes you are so absorbed in yourself, your problems, or your own agenda that you put yourself on auto-pilot and worry later just how you got wherever it was you were going, and how many lives you endangered along the way.

I had climbed up onto Hattie Peeler's porch and knocked on her front door before I realized that I could have been followed, that whoever it was that had Daisy's attention was a real threat, and was still out there waiting for me to make the wrong move. As I glanced behind me along Gas Line Road, I thought I saw someone leave the road and head into the park. But it was snowing just hard enough to keep me from seeing whether he walked with a limp. "Who's there?" Hattie said from behind the closed door.

"Garth Ryland. Let me in, Hattie, before you get us both shot."

Hattie opened the door to let me in. "I don't know

about you, but it would be a blessing to me," she said, opening the door and letting me inside.

Only one dim table lamp burned in Hattie's living room. All of her shades were drawn, and the rest of the house was completely dark. To anyone outside, it would appear that either she wasn't home or already had gone to bed.

"Where's Camelia?" I said to Hattie.

"I don't know what you're talking about."

"Yes, you do, or, as always, you'd have this place lit up like a Christmas tree."

Hattie wore a long white flannel nightgown, as if she really were dressed for bed, and white cotton booties that I guessed served as her house slippers. I followed her as far as her couch where we sat at opposite ends. To my left was her old floor model Philco radio that once could pull in stations as far away as Europe, although I didn't know if it still worked. Beside the radio, the mother of all ferns took up most of her east window, and on beyond it was Hattie's easy chair, footstool, and goose-necked floor lamp. The chair was where she did all of her reading, as evidenced by the stack of magazines on the footstool and in the magazine rack beside her chair.

"You and Ruth should get together," I said. "Between the two of you and what you pay for magazines, you could fund a library."

"You want them?" she said. "I've got no further use for them."

"No thanks. I've got an attic full now."

Camelia Capers came from the direction of Hattie's spare bedroom and stood in the arched doorway facing me. Her long black hair hung in a single braid to the middle of her back, and she wore jeans and a navy sweater that likely came from here in Oakalla. She also wore a pair of black tennis shoes and carried a large brown satchel in one hand and a small caliber revolver, probably a .22, in the other. Since she didn't smile in greeting, I imagined that the .22 was for my benefit.

"Put that gun down," Hattie said. "Garth's not here to hurt you."

But Camelia didn't put the gun down. Instead, she cleared the magazines off the foot stool and sat down on it with the satchel at her feet and her right hand, the one that held the .22, resting on her knee.

"That's as far as I go, Grandma," she said.

"That's far enough, I suppose," Hattie said. "Considering what you've been through."

As my glance went from grandmother to granddaughter, it confirmed the resemblance between them. Along with their shared eyes, nose, and cheekbones was a look of defiance that said, "Don't tread on me." The difference, I decided, was that one was born of confidence and the other born of fear. Both were great motivators, one sometimes the outgrowth of the other. But with fear you never knew when to stop running, whether for shelter, or to the top rung of the ladder—when enough was ever enough, no matter how much security surrounded you, or how many accolades fell your way.

Hattie nodded in the direction of the park. "Garth says there might be someone out there, Cammy. So you've been right all along."

"Larry Don?" I said.

Keeping one eye on me, Camelia went to the front door and raised the shade just enough for her to see out. Satisfied that she was safe for the moment, she sat back down on the footstool.

"Yes. Larry Don," she said as the life went out of her voice.

"How did you two happen to hook up anyway?"

She went to the east window, raised the blind and looked out, then sat back down again. If she kept it up, she was going to make me nervous.

"I blame my mother for that," she said with a southern accent as rich as Larry Don's. "Of course, I blame her for everything else that's wrong with me, so why not him. Emily Capers. Now, there's a study in still life."

"Don't be too hard on her," Hattie said. "She got what she wanted from life. With a little luck from now on, maybe you will, too."

"My mother is a God-damned fraud!" Camelia said in a voice on the edge of hysteria. "She turned her back on everything she was just so she could live the life a Southern belle. And then I came along. A junkie Indian of all things. Who didn't want to be a debutante, or a fucking Dixie Darling, or anything else she had planned for me." Camelia's eyes swept the room then came to an abrupt stop. I could almost feel their heat. "You asked me where I met Larry Don Loomus. He's the one who sold me the joint that got me busted there at Southern. Or gave it to me. Who knows. He and Joe Dan sometimes did favors for their regular customers."

"Joe Dan, as in Joe Dan Kidwell, alias Orion?" I said.

"Yes."

"They sold dope while they were both playing football?"

She laughed at my naiveté. "Dope or football, they were the main men on campus. If you wanted to score anything at all, it was no secret that you went to one of them."

"Did they use it as well?"

"On occasion maybe. I never saw either one of them use it, but there was hardly a time when they didn't have a beer in their hands and a woman on their arms. Not that there was any trick to that, being the studs they were."

She spoke without a trace of irony, as if it were yesterday, and nothing had happened in the interim to change her mind.

"You want to know the kicker?" she said. "Larry Don and Joe Dan were both at the same party where I got busted. They were arrested, but never charged."

"What happened after you got arrested?" I said, wondering if perhaps that was a turning point in her life. I could trace mine down to the very day, the very hour, the very minute my son died.

"Not much came of it. My daddy had been a professor there at Southern, so they slapped my wrist and gave me a year's probation."

"Was your father no longer with the university?"

She looked away with tears in her eyes. "Daddy died one day short of my 16th birthday. I've missed him each and every day since."

When she didn't offer an explanation, I looked to Hattie for help.

"Cammy's father was several years older than her mother," Hattie said. "He was 70 when he died."

"Professor Emeritus Benjamin Capers. How he loved the sound of that," Camelia said.

I thought I heard something brush softly against the house near the east window of the kitchen. But when I rose to check it out, Camelia pointed the .22 at me. I sat back down.

Camelia said, "My mother is the one who went apeshit over my probation. 'What would your father think? What must the neighbors think? Where or where have I gone wrong? Well, I'm not going to take this lying down. I have to do something, don't I?' From then on I was to live at home and check in and out with her every day. I couldn't see any of my former friends, and I wasn't allowed to date until she said so." Camelia laughed. Hers was a dry thin cackle with no belly to it. "As if my date had anything to do with it. He was about as straight arrow as they come. Oh, and two more things she'd forgot. I was to have a curfew. Nine p.m. on every day except Friday and Saturday, when I could stay out until eleven. And, I was to give her the keys to my car." Camelia shook her head at the folly of it all. "If she'd done that from the very start, it just might have worked. But for someone who'd been calling the shots since she was 12, it was a joke. I tried it all of a week before I left."

"To go where?"

"I didn't have a plan. But my first ride out of town was headed for Jackson, so that's where I ended up."

"Just like in the song," I said.

Her look said she didn't understand.

"Never mind. It was probably before your time."

"The problem was that when I got there, I didn't have any money, or any job, or any friends who could help me out. I was a spoiled rich bitch, up a creek without a paddle, as my first pimp put it."

"So you became a prostitute."

"Yes," she said, and left it at that.

I was relieved when Camelia got up to look outside. Somebody needed to be watching the store, and at the moment no one was.

"Are both doors locked?" I said to Hattie.

"With deadbolts."

"Good doors?"

"Same black walnut they've always been."

I nodded, though my stomach kept right on churning.

Camelia stood at the east window of the living room with the .22 in hand. Tall and model thin, she reminded me of a beautiful cardboard cutout, who would dance to the tune of every vagrant wind.

"After about four years of that, I hit bottom, deciding

that life, mine anyway, wasn't worth living anymore. So I took I don't know how many Valiums and went to bed, never intending to wake up. But wake up I did, and the first face I saw was that of my mother, looking down at me with this great big hurt in her eyes. Like here you go again, Camelia, ruining my life. What did I ever do to deserve a child like you?"

She sighed and sat down on the footstool. "From the hospital I went directly to Emerald City, where if they didn't do anything else for me, they cleaned me out. How? You're probably wondering. By putting me on a regular schedule of meals and exercise. By making me work for my room and board, and giving me extra money for the commissary only when I'd earned it. By not taking any of my lip, or letting me make excuses for why I couldn't do something. And by making me read every night about people who *had* done something with their lives, be it ever so humble. I suppose I was ready for all of that by then, which is why it worked, but I still couldn't have done it on my own."

"Then why did you leave?" I said.

"Boredom more than anything else. The first year was fine. I was learning who I was and who I wasn't and all I'd missed in life up until then. It was sort of like learning to walk all over again, and having my childhood back, which the drugs had stolen from me. But then I got restless. For what I didn't know. And I wanted out of there."

"But Orion wouldn't let you go?" I interrupted.

"No. He wouldn't. Because he knew that I knew who

he really was, and if I'd wanted to, I could blow the lid off the place. So I sneaked off into Chocsaw, which is a little cracker town a couple miles north of Emerald City, and went into the store there looking for a ride, when who should I meet coming out but Larry Don Loomus. He recognized me immediately. 'C.C.,' he said. 'How are you, darlin'?' Larry Don Loomus, as I live and breathe. You've got to get me out of here. 'Consider it done. Get in the truck.'"

She still seemed amazed at her good fortune. "That was all there was to it. I got in his pickup and went to live with Larry Don. I didn't learn until later what I had gotten myself into."

"It never occurred to you that it might have been a setup, that Joe Dan knew you were on the run and called Larry Don to intercept you?"

As she thought it over, I could see the wind leave her sails. "Not until now."

"What *had* you gotten yourself into?"

"A nest of cottonmouths, Larry Don being the king snake. The sonofabitch. Do you really think they set me up?"

"Finish what you started to tell me. Then you decide."

"The whole time that I was at Emerald City I had a hard time taking Joe Dan seriously as Orion. He'd let his hair grow really long and grown a beard and mustache and given up his whoring and his drinking, but what he reminded me of really, with his pale skin and blond hair and all, was a bleached-out Jesus wanna-be. Then when Larry Don told me what they were up to, it all made perfect sense."

201

"What were they up to?"

"Same old, same old, only on a much larger scale. Larry Don has been using Emerald City to launder his drug money ever since its beginning."

"Then why would Joe Dan now want to cut the strings and leave Larry Don hanging here in Oakalla?"

"I wasn't aware that he had. But if it's true, and Joe Dan really does want out, the only thing that comes to mind is that he's been reading his own press clippings, and come to believe he really is Orion."

"You mean *he's* starting to take himself seriously?"

"It sometimes happens."

For several seconds all was quiet there in the house. I listened for the knock on the door that I was sure was coming, but it never came.

"How does Larry Don launder his drug money through Emerald City?" I said.

"By giving it to Joe Dan, so he can give it back to Larry Don by buying land from him. You see, Emerald City sits on what used to be Larry Don's property. And most of the land that Orion is now buying up belongs to Larry Don, or his real estate clients. So since Emerald City is now fat city and the land around it keeps going up in price, Larry Don either gets a big commission, or the money outright from the sale of his own land. The problem as I see it, and maybe as Joe Dan now sees it, is that one of these days they're going to run out of land. What are they going to do then?"

"Is that why you left Larry Don?"

"Is that why you think I left?"

"No. I think you're running for your life. Aren't you?"

She took a deep breath, as the fear returned. "Yes. Before he broke his leg, Larry Don was an okay guy. I mean, he had it all. He was rich, good looking, staring a multi-million contract in the NFL right in the eye, plus who knows how much else in endorsements. 'Sugar,' he used to say to me. 'How many white running backs have you seen in the NFL lately? I'm going to be the next John Riggins.' But after he broke his leg, everything changed. It was like life said No to him for the very first time, and he couldn't take it."

"How did he change?" I said.

"He got mean for one thing. I didn't realize that until I hooked up with him again and saw how he operated. For another, everything had to be perfect or he'd get rid of it. He traded pickups every year, but if his new one would get so much as a scratch, he wouldn't fix it, but trade for another. Same with his boats and shotguns. Even his hired help had better not show up sick, or they'd be gone the next day. I remember he had this old pointer named Pronto Pup. He loved that old dog. He'd shot no end of birds over it. Well, one day Pronto Pup develops a limp because he's getting on and they've been hunting hard for several days. So they go out into the woods and Larry Don comes back alone. Where's Pronto Pup? I asked. 'I had to put him down.' Why? 'Because he couldn't cut the mustard any more.' About a week later I'm out walking in the woods, and I come across Pronto Pup, or what's left of him. Larry Don just shot him and let him lay where he fell." She shuddered. "I knew that was to be my fate one day, when he got tired of having me around. God forbid I sprain my ankle or grow a wrinkle in the meantime. But what gets me, and what I can't understand, is that there's not a damn thing wrong with Larry Don's leg. He only limps when he wants to."

"Say that again?" I said. "I thought he had a compound fracture."

"He did. He also had the best bone surgeon in the South operate on his leg and put it back together again. The only thing that kept Larry Don from trying out for the NFL was his fear of it happening again."

That didn't come as good news. "Could Larry Don, say, walk a railroad rail if he wanted?" I said.

"He could walk a rail fence if he wanted. I know because I've seen him do it."

"Could he live in the woods for a few days if he chose?"

"I don't see why not. He can do about anything that he sets his mind to."

"I've underestimated him."

She shrugged as if it were no big deal. "People usually do. To their everlasting regret," she felt compelled to add.

"Then how did you get away from him?"

"I haven't yet," she reminded me.

"This far anyway?"

"Because, for whatever the reason, he trusted me. Whenever a drug deal would go down, Larry Don would have me drive that old black pickup of his, while he would ride shotgun. For real. He never carried a sidearm. He always carried a double-barreled shotgun with a bunch of extra shells in his pockets." She opened her hand to show me the .22. "He had this in with the money, but that was for me more than anything else, in case something went wrong and he couldn't make it back to the pickup. He said that way I could always shoot myself before they could have their way with me."

"Thoughtful of him."

"Yes. I thought so."

I studied her face, again saw no irony there. Then I realized why Camelia Capers had been such an easy mark, and probably would remain so, even if she survived the night, which was beginning to look doubtful for any of us there. Some people, no matter what hand life deals them, never lose their innocence. They can be lied to, beaten up, double-crossed, and put down, but they go on believing that with just a little more love or luck they'll do better next time. Camelia appeared to be one of those people. However, in fairness to saints the world over, innocence should never be confused with goodness.

Camelia said, "The way it always went down, we would drive to the airstrip there on Larry Don's cattle ranch and wait for the plane to land. After it had landed and the Mexicans had gotten out, Larry Don would get out and go taste the stuff before he'd even let the money leave the truck. If he got into any kind of trouble, my instructions were to get out of there as best I could, and he'd take care of himself, meeting me back at the house later . . . if there was a later. If all was well, he'd signal to me and I'd drive up with the money, which we'd exchange for the dope."

"How much money?"

She patted the satchel at her feet. "A million dollars."

"That's not chump change."

She didn't smile. "No. Not at all. But this last time when Larry Don signaled me that all was well, I hit the brights and the accelerator at the same time and, except for the gas I stole along the way, didn't stop until I got to Oakalla."

"And got shot for your troubles."

"Yes. One of the bullets nicked my side. I'd lost a lot of blood by the time I got here."

"But all we found were slugs. Why didn't we find any shotgun pellets?"

"That's because Larry Don didn't shoot at me."

"You have an explanation why?"

She did, but didn't appear to like it. "I think he wanted me to escape. I think he wanted to have to come after me. He's getting bored with his life. Man-hunting, or in this case woman-hunting, that's a whole new challenge."

"I thought he was a private detective."

"In name only. He keeps a dummy office in New Orleans, but that's only to cover his tail for all the trips he makes around the country."

"Then how did he know to come here?"

"Because early on, when he met me in that store, he

asked me where I was headed. Oakalla, I said. 'Florida?' No, Wisconsin. It was the one place that I could go where I knew they'd take me in, no questions asked. I was lucky, he said. He'd never had a place like that."

"And the pickup you stole? If Larry Don likes everything all new and shiny, how do you explain it?"

"His daddy bought it for him for Larry Don's 16th birthday. He says he drank his first six-pack and got his first piece of ass in that truck, both on the same night. But he didn't keep it around for sentimental reasons. He kept it around because he filed the serial numbers off about the time he got heavy into the dope business and didn't license it after that. That way if he ever had to ditch it, say during a drug raid, it wouldn't come back on him."

"And the DEA agent who disappeared from Emerald City a while back?"

"I don't know anything about that," she said, protecting herself. "But I do know about a bundle that Larry Don asked the Mexicans to drop off for him on their way home over the Gulf. The bundle that was kicking and squirming in the back of the pickup at the time." She rose and picked up the satchel. "Which is likely to be my fate, if Larry Don ever gets his hands on me."

"Where are you going?" I said.

"Out the back door. If Larry Don's watching the front, at least I'll have a running start."

She didn't sound as if she liked her odds. Knowing what I did about Larry Don, I didn't like them either.

"There's a deer head on the hood of the pickup," I said. "Be advised of that."

"Larry Don's work. His way of advertising what to expect when he catches me."

"We can make a phone call. Try to get some help here."

"No. For two reasons. If that's Larry Don out there, the line's already been cut. If it's not, I don't plan on sharing this money with anyone."

"Don't you have a cell phone?" I didn't, but some people did.

She reached into her pocket and held it up to show me. "No bars inside the house."

"One last question," I said, knowing that I couldn't keep her there any longer and that it might be my last chance ever to talk to her. "Did you steal ten dollars worth of gas from Fickle Store Sunday night?"

"Yes. But unless you can break a hundred, I'll just have to owe him."

That answered another question as to why she stole the gas instead of paying for it. A bloody woman with a hundred dollar bill in a pickup with no license plate might arouse suspicion.

"You did know that Fickle Store burned down Monday night?" I said.

"Grandma told me. But I didn't do it."

"Could Larry Don have, then burned down the church to flush you out?"

"He could have. But I don't think he did. It's not his style."

"What is his style?"

She started through the kitchen for the back door. "Pray to God you never find out."

Chapter 20

"Why a computer, for God's sake?" I said.

Hattie and I stood at her back door. Already I had tried the phone, but as Camelia predicted, it was dead. So was Hattie's computer, which was tied to the phone line.

Hattie said, "So I could play video poker. It sure beats solitaire by a country mile."

"Here I go. If I make it out of the yard alive, head for the nearest phone and call the state police, not 911. I don't want Cecil involved. He might get himself shot."

"You can't save her from herself, Garth. I'm not sure anyone can. And she's lying about breaking a hundred dollar bill. I gave her plenty of traveling money."

"The way you lied about the pickup going east out of town? You *are* the one who hid it in Beezer's corncrib, aren't you?"

"For the good it did. It sounds like Larry Don found it anyway."

"Not your fault."

"It will be if you get yourself killed."

"I'm going to try very hard to avoid that." I went out the back door on the run.

———————

A snowball's chance in hell, I thought, on my way through the yard with only a few stray flakes for cover. But the fast rising wind at my back changed all that. Like an arctic dam burst, it smashed through the trees bordering the clover field, gathering a snow cloud ahead of it. This it flung across the field, as it raced ahead to scoop another cloud of snow. Blinded by the first volley, when the whole field seemed to explode in white, I could only stand in awe of it. But when the next gust came, I was ready.

The corncrib where the pickup sat was down a hill in a clearing about 50 yards ahead. Although I had not heard the boom of Larry Don's shotgun, neither had I seen any sign of the pickup. If Camelia had made it that far, she should have been on her way out by now.

I moved slowly down the hill through the scrub oak, as the wind tossed their branches and fanned their leaves into such a fury that I could neither see, nor hear, nor think, and left me at the mercy of a bad case of nerves. So when the moon momentarily peeked out from behind a cloud and washed the hill in light, I instinctively hit the ground and began to crawl. I didn't know why, whether crawl was better than crouch, or down better than up. One thing seemed certain, however; if Larry Don were waiting for me in the barn, my present course was suicide.

I stopped several feet short of the clearing while trying to decide what to do next. There at the bottom of the hill the wind was kept partially at bay by the hill itself, and I could see that except for what the wind blew from the trees, the snow had all but stopped. As the stragglers flitted about the corncrib, like the moths of summer, I was taken by how idyllic the scene—white flakes against the weathered gray wood of the corncrib, a white-crested stand of jack pines at the edge of a meadow only a few yards away. If my number came up tonight, I guessed that there were worse places to die.

"Larry Don, you in there?" I shouted at the corncrib.

His answer was to blow the bush to my right to kingdom come. But I didn't move. A hunter's eye is trained to movement, and he had another barrel left.

"Where's Camelia?" I tried again.

"C.C. is asleep in the truck."

"Alive or dead?"

"Very much alive, thank you."

The bush to my left went next. Larry Don didn't realize that I had hunkered down behind a granite boulder that would have taken a bazooka's best shot.

I waited for him to reload, then said, "What do you plan to do with her?"

"Take her back home to Mississippi with me."

"And after that?"

"See how well she can swim."

The top of the boulder seemed to explode, as I was showered with snow and bits of rock. No question about it, he was getting the range.

"Is that necessary?" I said. "You have your money. Why not take it and go in peace?"

"Because that's not the way I operate, Mr. Ryland. I trusted C.C. and she let me down. That's not something I can forgive, or forget."

"What about Joe Dan? He let you down too?"

"Sad to say, he did. That's another matter I must attend to once I get home."

"If you get home."

"Oh, I will, Mr. Ryland. You are the last obstacle in my way."

The boulder exploded again, as another round of debris showered me. Very soon, he would figure out just exactly what the situation was.

"You're hiding behind something, aren't you?" he said right on cue.

"Larry Don, you are a master of the obvious."

"The question is, are you armed?"

"Why don't you come out of the corncrib and find out?"

"I'm already out of the corncrib, and since you have yet to fire a round, I must assume you are unarmed."

I chanced a glance in his direction. He was right on both counts. He was five yards outside the corncrib, and I didn't have so much as a peashooter. All of my hopes rested on an ace in the hole.

"You see, I had it all figured out, Mr. Ryland," he said as he started walking toward me. "I knew C.C. must eventually come here, as I knew you would eventually lead me to her. Remember I told you that you were a man of discipline, a man who knew how to hold his block. You took it as a compliment and in a backhanded way it is, but what I really meant was that you're predictable. You can always be counted on to finish what you start, and you always try to do the right thing, no matter what the cost to you. Like coming here tonight unarmed to try to save C.C. Stupid, yet honorable, like all those fine sons of the South who charged up Cemetery Ridge. But I'm part of the new South, Mr. Ryland. And honor doesn't mean a damn thing to me."

"Aren't you forgetting something?" I said, my ace in the hole starting to look like a joker.

"You mean that old woman back at the house, who at this very minute is calling the authorities down on me? I thought of her, too. That's what I want her to do. While they're racing out here to save you, C.C. and I will be walking the railroad tracks back to town. By the time they find your body, we'll be long gone."

He was only a few feet away at the edge of the clearing. I gathered myself for what I knew would be a fatal charge. But I'd be damned if I'd give him the satisfaction of my running away.

"You see, Mr. Ryland, I was junior national trap shoot champion three years running. Once I flush you out from behind that rock, you're a dead man."

A sudden fierce gust of wind swept down upon us, seemed even to shake the boulder behind which I sat. I saw Larry Don stagger as both barrels of his shotgun fired one right after the other into the ground. Then he whirled and disappeared into a shower of snow.

It wasn't until I saw Beezer approach with his .30-.30 Winchester that I moved out from behind the boulder. Beezer's face was blackened with soot, and he wore a black stocking cap pulled all the way down to his eyebrows and a camouflaged hunting vest over his coveralls. He was indeed a sight for sore eyes.

Silently we followed Larry Don's bloody trail toward the small creek to the south. There at the edge of the creek, his right foot entangled in a greenbrier, we found Larry Don hanging upside down over the bank, his shotgun still in his hand.

He reminded me of the hunting dog that I had seen hanging from a fence while canoeing down Owl Creek a few years ago. I thought then, I thought now—a hell of a way to die.

I climbed down the bank to check Larry Don's pulse. He had none.

"He dead?" Beezer said, as he kicked Larry Don's boot just to make sure.

"As a doornail."

"I was aiming for his heart. I must've hit his lungs."

"Where were you hiding?"

In Larry Don's coat pocket, I found several twelve gauge double O shotgun shells, along with a roll of duct tape. I could only guess the intended use of the duct tape, but imagined it was for Camelia on her ride back to Mississippi in the trunk of Larry Don's rental car. I climbed back up the bank and brushed the snow off of me. Larry Don would have to wait for whoever arrived next on the scene to free him from the greenbrier.

Beezer pointed to show me where he'd been hiding. "In that cluster of scrub oaks. Somebody years ago had built a tree stand there. I figured I might as well use it."

"You've been waiting here all along?"

We walked toward the corncrib. I hoped that Larry Don was as good as his word and that Camelia was still alive.

"From day one after Old Elmo was killed. That really got my go button, Garth. I heard the shot and got out here as fast as I could, but it was too late to save him. His head was already on the hood of that truck in there. Who could have done such a thing, I wondered? Killed such a magnificent animal, used his head as a hood ornament, and then left the rest of him to rot? And avoided me in the process, which is no mean feat. Not somebody I wanted running loose in my woods. So I decided to stake this place out and see what might happen. But until tonight, you were my only customer."

"He came and went the night the church burned."

"Was that what all of the commotion was about? I was up in my cabin when it happened."

"You were the one who kept your cabin warm?" I said.

"By building small fires that wouldn't give me away."

We stopped in front of the corncrib. All was quiet inside. Even the wind seemed to be taking a break.

"And that was your shelter and campfire I found in the woods?"

"Yes."

"Why then didn't I find any of your tracks?"

"Because, Garth, an Apache couldn't follow me through a snowdrift if I didn't want him to. I grew up in the woods, remember? Lived most of my life there."

What happened next took us by surprise. Just as we entered the corncrib, the pickup started, its one headlight came on and fixed us momentarily in its glare, like the eye of Cyclops, and then with a roar it sprang at us. Beezer dived to the right. I dived to the left, and somehow the pickup missed both of us, as it crossed the clearing, throwing snow as it gathered speed.

"She'll never make it up the hill," Beezer said as I pulled him to his feet.

"I bet she does."

I was right. She did make it up the hill. The last we saw of her was the pickup's taillights when it entered the alfalfa field. After that we saw only the hole in the trees through which she had gone.

"I'll be damned." Beezer was as still as a statue.

"Make that a double."

With nothing more to do there, I walked with Beezer back to his cabin. I had just stepped onto Gas Line Road and started home when the fire siren rang.

Chapter 21

They were loading Michelle Gustavson into the Operation Lifeline ambulance when I arrived at the parsonage. Carrying what looked like a bed sheet folded in her arms, Janie was about to climb into the ambulance with her daughter. Not knowing how serious the situation was, I said to Janie, "Want me to ride along?"

She grabbed my hand and pulled me up into the ambulance with her. I guessed that meant yes.

I sat on the floor. Janie stood beside the gurney, holding Michelle's hand, as the young paramedic there in the back with us looked on. Since they weren't trying to treat Michelle, I had three choices. She was either dead, or out of danger, or had a concussion, as it appeared to me. If she had a concussion, that would delay treatment until they got her to the hospital and found out what was going on inside her head.

The wind, which had nearly frozen me on my way

into town, was relentless. At the last streetlight on Madison Road just before we left town, a gust struck the ambulance with such force that for an instant I thought that we were all headed for the ditch. But the driver fought her way through it and delivered us safely to the Adams County Hospital's emergency room.

The paramedics wheeled Michelle inside, as Janie gave the woman at the desk all the vital information, such as name, occupation, and HMO. Though the woman tried to be reassuring, I could tell that Janie was too worried to be bothered.

"Can't some of this wait until later?" I said.

The woman, whose name was Joan, said, "I suppose so."

Janie was out of her chair in a flash. "I'm going to check on Michelle," she said. "Here. Hold this." She handed me the bed sheet she'd been carrying.

I gave her a questioning look.

"It's my robe," she said. "I forgot I had it with me."

Not just any robe, I decided as I carried it into the waiting room, but her ministerial robe. Soft white linen with beautiful gold embroidery, it felt cool and soothing to touch.

You think that you will never ever forget, but you do. The year that my son was in and out of the hospital a dozen different times, the last time for good, I thought that I would never forget what it was like. I thought that I would never forget the pain, the always and endless uncertainty that kept me up nights listening for his every breath and filled every watchful hour with prayer; the sparkles of hope that I gathered like gold dust because they were so precious, so few. I would never forget the taste of luke-warm Vienna sausages, fresh from the vending machine, cheese-and-crackers eaten on the run, the empty feel of a hospital canteen when in the wee hours of the morning, I was the first, last, and only one in line. Or even the look, taste, smell, and feel of a hospital itself. I forgot, and then on a cold and blustery night in November, I remembered-why I don't, never ever will again, like hospitals.

Cecil, hat in hand, smelling strongly of smoke, sat down in the hard red plastic chair beside me. His shirt starched, his uniform pressed, he looked remarkably refreshed compared to me. But after sleeping all day, he should have.

"Pardon me saying so, Garth, but you look like something the cat drug in."

"I feel like something the cat drug in, Cecil. What's up?"

"I just wondered how Michelle is doing?"

"We should know in a few minutes. Her mother is checking on her now."

"Then you can fill me in later."

He made a motion as if he were about to rise, but I noticed that he still sat where he was. "Was there something else, Cecil?"

"I need to talk to Reverend Gustavson, but maybe you can do that for me."

"What about?"

"Her daughter."

"What about her daughter?"

"I hate to say this, Garth, but I think that she might have started the fire."

"Go ahead. I'm on company time."

Cecil shifted nervously in his seat as he checked the doorway to make sure that Janie wasn't on her way into the waiting room. "Well, as you know, I've been sleeping days so that I could stay out on the streets all night. And let me tell you, just two days down the road, it's been an eye opener. Do you know that Wilmer Wiemer is up most of the night roaming the town? The same Wilmer Wiemer that owns half of Adams County?"

I smiled at him. "The stories I could tell you, Cecil."

"Well, it was news to me. Anyway, I was on patrol coming east on Maple Street with my lights off when I saw someone dart out of the alley there beside the phone company, cross the street, and take off running down the sidewalk in the same direction that I was headed. She didn't stop for School Street, but went flying across it as if it weren't there. I made a California stop myself, but somehow lost her in the process. So I went on by the parsonage and the church, turned right on Fickle Road, then right again when I came to the school. Another right onto School Street put me back where I'd lost her. I was about to circle the block all over again, when I saw the fire in the basement of the parsonage. Fooled me at that, even though fire is all I've had on my mind lately. I almost drove by it, thinking it was a light reflecting in the basement window from somewhere."

"Lucky you didn't," Janie said from the door of the waiting room. "Or Michelle and I would both be dead."

Cecil and I stood as Janie approached.

"Well, I'd better get going," Cecil said.

"Not without a hug first."

Cecil stood stiff as a scarecrow as Janie hugged him, then kissed him lightly on the cheek.

"I take it Michelle's going to be okay?" I said.

"*Yes*," she said with a smile that enveloped all of us. "She has a concussion and it will probably be morning before she awakens. But they did an MRI, and the doctor assured me that she's going to be fine." She hugged Cecil again. "Thanks to this man here."

"So tell me about it," I said to him.

"Some other time."

Embarrassed, a red-faced Cecil was trying hard to leave. But Janie had him by the hand and wouldn't let go.

"Michelle and I were both on the stairs when Marshal Hardwick found us. She had fallen on the stairs, and I had tripped over her on my way down. He carried me out then went after her. A few more minutes in there, and the smoke would have killed us."

"There was one casualty, though," Cecil said to get out of the limelight. "I wrecked the front door getting in."

"A small price to pay," Janie said, as she finally let go of him.

"And the rest of the parsonage?" I said.

Cecil donned his hat and made sure he put some distance between us before he answered. "The fire stayed in the basement. But as Reverend Gustavson said, there was an awful lot of smoke in there."

"I guess that's good news," I said.

Seeing his chance, Cecil left.

———————————

"Is there anything I can get you?" I asked Janie.

We sat side by side in the hard red plastic chairs. She had a pack of Marlboro 100s in her hand, but confronted by the large No Smoking sign overhead, had yet to light one.

"How about a new life? Mine seems to suck right about now."

"You still have your daughter."

She slipped the cigarettes into the pocket of her sweatshirt. "For which I'll be eternally grateful."

I took her hand in mine. She rested her head on my shoulder. "Want to tell me about the fire?" I said.

"There's not much to tell."

"I'd still like to hear it." I needed to know what Cecil had left unsaid.

She pulled away from me. "Why?"

"Because if it's arson, we need to get to the bottom of it."

"Oh," she said, resting her head on my shoulder again. "I never thought of that."

"Maybe you should think of it."

"What do you mean?"

"The church, now the parsonage. The fact that Michelle thought she saw a man running away from the church the night of the fire. Maybe somebody is out to get you."

"I wouldn't know who."

"What about Wild Bill?"

Her hand tightened on mine. "He hates that name. It followed him everywhere we went."

"I'm not surprised."

"What about? His hating it or the fact it followed him?"

"Either one. It's not often a minister kills someone."

"It was self-defense. He had no other choice."

"But it might have left him bitter when he didn't get the appointments he wanted and probably deserved."

"It did. But I had nothing to do with that. I supported him every step of the way. Besides, he would never do anything that would endanger Michelle. He loves her too much." She pulled away again to make sure I understood. "I mean that."

"What if he thought she wouldn't be there tonight?"

"She wasn't there tonight. She was spending the night with a friend."

"Then how did she end up on the stairs?"

"I don't know. I'll have to ask her in the morning. I was in my room with the door closed reading my Bible." Her look wasn't exactly flattering. "And because I know you'll ask, the reason the door was closed is because Michelle keeps it like an iceberg up there, and it's a lot warmer with the door closed. And I had my robe in my lap because it's my security blanket, what I hold on to whenever I'm afraid, and I'm afraid now . . . of a lot of things. Then I heard a door bang and Michelle running across the living room yelling MOM! I laid the Bible down and opened my bedroom door, when I was hit by what seemed like a wall of smoke rushing into the room. We have a smoke detector on the stairs. I don't know why it didn't go off, but it didn't. So I came running down the stairs looking for Michelle, and that's all I remember until I was sitting on the porch and Marshall Hardwick was carrying Michelle out the front door."

"Did Michelle have any reason to think that you wouldn't be home tonight?" I said.

Janie didn't like the question but chose to answer it. "I did tell her that since she wouldn't be there, I might go visit a friend in Madison just to get away for a while. Why is that important, though, if you think it's Wild Bill who is out to get me?"

"Just checking all the possibilities."

"No. In a roundabout way, you were checking to see if Michelle thought the coast was clear when she decided to burn down the parsonage."

"I have my reasons," I said, not liking where we were headed.

"I'd like to hear them."

I didn't want to tell her. But I felt that it probably was already the end of us no matter what I did. Janie would fight like hell to protect her one chick, regardless of who was in the wrong.

"In the first place, I've never bought that story of Michelle's that she saw a man running away from the church on the night of the fire . . ."

"Why not?" Janie interrupted. "Isn't it possible that someone besides Michelle might want to burn down the church, someone with a grievance against it, who, in your own words, 'had his sacred innocence sullied by its indifference?'"

"I said that?"

"You know damn well you did."

"Then it would appear I'm wrong about Michelle."

"Yes, you are."

"Except that there is a double row of Lombardy poplars between the parsonage and the church, and though their leaves are now gone, the trees are still there."

"She could have seen through them."

"Not likely. Then there was the FBI agent she sicced on me. Why would she do that if she had nothing to hide?"

"She didn't do that. I did. Unintentionally, but I did. I happened to mention to Agent Stevenson when he talked to us that we had been over the same ground with you, and if he didn't mind my saying so, you were by far the better investigator. Since you went about things so casually, almost like a friend, one hardly noticed when the knife went in, or when you took it out again."

She had started to cry. I felt like joining her.

"I am your friend, Janie. Believe it if you will."

"I don't. And as for your insinuations that Michelle set fire to the church and parsonage, I have to ask you. What could possibly be her motive?"

"Her father."

"What about him?"

"Michelle hinted to me that there might be problems there."

"What kind of problems? Because if you think he's been abusing her, you're way off base. Wild Bill Gustavson is a lot of things but he's not a child abuser."

"You're sure of that?"

"Absolutely. I know all the signs. I've been trained in these things, remember? I *am* a minister, regardless of what you might think of my abilities."

"Okay. I'm wrong about Michelle."

"Please say it like you mean it."

"If you'll tell me, with the same absolute certainty, that Michelle never left the parsonage Monday night."

"What happened Monday night?"

"Fickle Store burned down."

"Why would Michelle want to burn down Fickle Store?"

"I don't know. Maybe for practice."

Her look said that this time I'd stepped way too far over the line. "Garth, if you really are my friend, you'll stop right there."

But I wasn't ready to stop yet because we hadn't gotten

227

at the truth. "You said yourself that Michelle isn't happy here in Oakalla. Without a church and a parsonage, maybe she wouldn't have to live here anymore."

"Even if that were true, why Fickle Store? She's never even been in there that I know of."

"She's never partied at Coon Lake, never had a friend that died in a car wreck on his way home from there?" Although that had happened two years in the past, sometimes the past could jump up and bite us when we least expected it.

I didn't know how to interpret her silence, whether I'd scored a bullseye or not. Then she held out both hands. "My robe, please."

Reluctantly I handed it to her. As she had earlier, I'd forgotten that I was even holding it.

"I'm sorry, Janie. I really am."

Tears welled up in her eyes. She used the robe to blot them out. "So am I, Garth. I thought we had something good going, you and I."

"It doesn't have to end here."

Her face went stone hard. "Yes, Garth. I'm afraid it does."

CHAPTER 22

On my way back to town the wind reminded me why there are so many cases of frostbite in Wisconsin every winter. You think you are dressed warmly enough in your thick lined gloves, wool stocking cap, and sheepherder's coat, but tell that to your feet—hiking boots and one pair of cotton socks (sans Gore Tex), when your toes go numb.

Then I saw a pair of headlights coming my way. It was with the greatest relief that I opened the passenger door and climbed inside Cecil's patrol car.

"With the wind chill, it feels like it's 20 below out there," Cecil said. "That's what the weatherman said."

"He must be in Miami Beach," I said as I pulled off my boots and began rubbing my toes back to life. "Is this as high as the heat will go?"

Cecil turned the fan up a couple more notches. "How's that?"

"Better."

With great care to avoid the ditch on either side, Cecil turned the Impala around in the road. As he did, I could feel the wind buffet the car, as if trying to push it over the edge. I shuddered to think that I could still be out there.

"The state police found a body out in Beezer's woods. You know anything about that?" he said.

I put my boots back on then wiggled my toes to make sure that I still could. "It's Larry Don Loomus. He's the owner of the pickup that started all of this."

"And that deer head they found in the snow? I'm sure you'll get around to telling me about it, too."

"It belongs to Old Elmo."

"Of course, Old Elmo."

We stopped at the four-way stop there in front of the shelter and across from the United Methodist Church. I kept my eyes straight ahead so as not to look at either one. Each in its own way had been my refuge, and now each of them was gone.

"Somebody took the battery out of the smoke-detector," Cecil said.

"What's that, Cecil?" I heard, but wasn't really listening.

"The parsonage. Somebody had taken the battery out of the smoke-detector there at the foot of the stairs. That's why it never went off."

"Who would do that?" I said to get his opinion.

"Michelle is my guess. What's yours?"

"Same as yours. But her mother swears that Michelle had nothing to do with the fire."

We stopped at the intersection of Jackson Street and School Street then went on. Home Street had never looked so good to me. More than once that night I'd thought that I might never see it again.

"Did her mother explain then why the front door was locked when I tried to get in?" Cecil said as he stopped the Impala in front of my house. "Why I had to break the glass to get in at all?"

"No. She didn't explain that."

"Somebody should. If Michelle went in the front door like I think she did, why would she, seeing the hurry that she was in, turn around and lock it behind her? You tell me that, Garth."

"Maybe she didn't go in the front door. Maybe she went in the back," I said, playing the devil's advocate. "Can you be sure she went in the front door?"

"No. But it seems reasonable, seeing that's where she was headed." He gave me a long questioning look. "Whose side are you on, anyway?"

"Yours, Cecil. But right now I'm trying to give Michelle the benefit of every doubt."

"I suppose there's a reason for that."

I reached for the door handle to let myself out. "Her mother makes a pretty strong case in Michelle's defense."

"Any mother worth her salt would."

"True. But now she has me wondering."

"I hope that's your head talking, and not your heart."

"I hope so too, Cecil. Good night."

231

"Something to sleep on, Garth. Danny found a burned-out two-gallon gas can in the basement. Thought you'd like to know."

"Larry Don would have made it, Ruth," I said. "The fire would have been his cover."

Ruth had fixed a fresh pot of coffee shortly before I arrived home. I filled my cup half full of Old Crow, then after adding sugar and half-and-half, filled it the rest of the way with coffee. It wasn't something that I would recommend to a connoisseur of either bourbon or Irish coffee. But what the hell. It warmed me up inside.

"What are you talking about?" Ruth said. Though dressed for bed in her housecoat and moccasins, she had made no move in that direction.

"Larry Don Loomus. He had it planned so that when Camelia made her move on the pickup, he would ambush her there, carry her and the money along the railroad as far as Fickle Road then pick them up on his way out of town. With everyone at the fire at the parsonage, chances are he would have made it."

"What stopped him?"

"Beezer Portnoy."

"I thought that you thought Beezer was dead."

"That's what he wanted us to think." I took a drink of Garth's Original Irish coffee, and sighed in contentment as it burned all the way down. "But I was never quite convinced." Then I went on to tell her how my night had gone.

"Maybe the girl *is* telling you the truth," Ruth said when I'd finished. "Maybe she really did see a man leaving the church."

"That's why I've got to call Clarkie soon. When I can make myself get up."

I felt welded to my chair. The bourbon had sapped my last remaining strength. I wouldn't go out again that night, even if our house were on fire.

"Why Clarkie?" Ruth said.

"I need William Gustavson's phone number and figure that he's the only one who can get it for me in short order."

"Can't it wait until tomorrow?"

"It could. But I might be out of the mood by then."

Ruth took a piece of paper out of her purse and sailed it across the table to me. "You can call Clarkie if you like, but that's William Gustavson's number right there. I figured you might need it before this was all over."

"Ruth, you're a peach," I said.

Her look was wistful. "Karl used to say that to me."

"Then I'm in good company."

"Good enough."

I made myself get up from the table and go to the phone. Wild Bill was likely already in bed, and under any circumstance he would not welcome my phone call, but he still needed to know that his daughter was in the hospital, and why.

I had to let it ring five times and was about to give up when a man with unmistakable power and assurance in his voice answered. Wild Bill. It had to be.

"Reverend Gustavson?"

"Yes. Who is this?"

"Garth Ryland. I heard you speak years ago."

"The same Garth Ryland whose column I used to enjoy? Oakalla, isn't it?"

"Yes."

"Which is where my daughter, Michelle, is living now."

We hadn't been on the phone 30 seconds and already he was two steps ahead of me. This wasn't going to be easy. Any of it.

"That's why I called, Reverend Gustavson. Michelle is in the hospital with a concussion, but is expected to fully recover. I thought you'd want to know."

"I'll be on a plane yet tonight."

Damn, I thought. I've already lost him.

"Reverend Gustavson, could you answer a couple questions first? As I said, Michelle's in no danger."

"Then why can't your questions wait until tomorrow?"

"It's the circumstances under which she got hurt. There's been a fire. Three of them actually, within the past week. With two of them Michelle has been very close to the action."

"How close?"

"She called the first one in. That was the church. Tonight it was the parsonage. She fell and hit her head while running up the stairs to rescue her mother."

"And her mother?" No mistaking the concern in his voice.

"She's fine. But they both had to be carried out of the parsonage. It was a close call, Reverend Gustavson."

"All the more reason for me to leave now."

"Just one more thing. Why is Michelle unhappy with you at this point in time?"

"I divorced her mother. That's reason enough."

"It seems to go beyond that."

"It does. But it's not what you're thinking."

"What am I thinking, Reverend Gustavson?"

"That there's something improper between Michelle and me. And while you're dead wrong, considering today's moral climate and what has happened with Michelle, I can't much blame you. However, the reason that Michelle and I are feuding is much more innocent than that. She thinks my present wife is too old for me. Michelle calls her Granny, though not to her face of course."

"How old is she?"

"Sixty-five. My age."

"And the reason you left the ministry?"

"I didn't leave it. I retired to Florida. But that didn't last a year before I took on a church down here."

"I'm sorry. I owe you an apology. You and Michelle both."

"Then make sure she receives it."

"I will. Good night."

"Good night, Mr. Ryland. I'll look forward to speaking to you in the morning, in case you have any more questions."

He hung up. A few seconds later I did the same.

"I struck out," I said to Ruth. "For the second time tonight."

"What was the first?"

"Janie Gustavson. I'm no longer on her short list."

"You didn't tell me you were on her list at all, or that you wanted to be." Her look was designed to extract as much guilt as she could. "Though I'm not surprised."

"I get lonely sometimes, Ruth."

"Then do what I do. Go bowling with your friends."

"My friends don't bowl. Either one of them."

"Then find some new friends, is my suggestion. Ones that won't tempt you to do what you shouldn't."

"What would be the fun in that?"

She just shook her head. She knew that I was beyond help where women were concerned.

"But to ease your mind, Ruth, nothing happened that shouldn't have between Janie and me. And now, thanks to my inquiring mind, it never will."

"Then thank your lucky stars and go on. The last thing you need is another bird with a broken wing."

"Diana, you mean, as the first one?"

"Who else? Now that she's finally out of your life, for God's sake don't go back into the fire again."

"Poor choice of words, Ruth. Considering."

"Not to my way of thinking."

"Are you not so subtly trying to tell me something?"

"Think about it, Garth, all that's burned down around here lately."

I thought about it, but didn't see where she was headed. "A church, a parsonage, a grocery store. Why?"

"Think about it some more."

"What's to think about, Ruth?" I said, too tired to make the effort. "The church and the parsonage, yes. I can make a connection there, though I'm not sure what anymore. But Fickle Store? Now, if it were a church, you might have something."

"You mean you really don't know?" She was surprised at me.

"Know what?"

"Fickle Store *was* a church originally. Jasper Peterson bought it and made it into a grocery store after his first store burned down."

The news hit me like a thunderbolt. I wondered where the church had gone, but always assumed that they'd razed it along with the rest of the buildings in Fickle that had disappeared in my absence. "A church, you say."

"Yes. A United Methodist Church, it was by then. On a yoked charge with Oakalla."

"You mean the same minister served both churches?"

"Yes. That's what I mean."

"Then the man who drowned in Coon Lake would have served both places."

"Reverend Israel Hammond."

"You don't happen to have his wife's phone number, do you?"

"No. But I can get it for you."

"Would you, please."

"It means I have to call Beulah Peters and get her out of bed."

"Whatever it takes, Ruth."

While Ruth made the phone call, I went to the front door and looked outside. The wind met me there with a gust that shook the house and that I could feel through two panes of glass. The thought of going out into it again was almost more than I could bear.

"Garth?" Ruth said from behind me. "I've got what you wanted." And when I didn't respond, "Garth? Did you hear me?"

"I heard you, Ruth. But part of me doesn't want to know."

"The best part, probably."

I went into the dining room and dialed the number that she had given me.

"Hello?" A thin guarded voice said. Already I didn't like Betty Hammond, but it had nothing to do with the sound of her voice.

"Is this Betty Hammond?"

"Yes. Who is this? You realize how late it is, don't you?"

"Yes. And I wouldn't call except that we have something of an emergency here and I need your help."

"What kind of help? If it's money you want, I'm a widow on a fixed income."

"It's not money, Mrs. Hammond. This call is about your late husband, Reverend Israel Hammond."

"What about Israel?" she was stridently defiant. "He was a good God-fearing man, who died in the faith, so I'll hear no voice raised against him."

"Don't hang up, Mrs. Hammond," I pleaded. "I have no questions about your husband, only where he served." I picked up the envelope on which I'd written Clarkie's list of churches recently destroyed by fire. I said, "Tell me if your late husband served either or both of these churches. Olarno United Methodist, Wheatville United Methodist."

"Mrs. Hammond?" I said, hearing nothing from her and thinking that she had hung up on me.

"Both of them. He also served at Oakalla and Boynette, though it is my understanding that Boynette is a community church now."

I looked down at my list. Boynette Community Church was on it.

"And do you have a daughter named Janie Gustavson?"

"Yes," she snapped. "But we haven't spoken for years."

"Is that because your late husband was abusing her, or because she killed him, or both?"

Click.

"I had to ask," I said in the face of Ruth's disapproval.

"I suppose you did. But I doubt that Beulah Peters will agree."

"Since when did you start worrying about what Beulah Peters thinks?"

"You're right. It's too late to start now."

I'd put on my coat and stocking cap and was already at the back door when she said, "What makes you think Janie Gustavson was abused by her father?"

"It was a guess, Ruth. But why else would she try

to destroy everything in her past that reminded her of him?"

"And the part about killing him?"

"Just a hunch. I won't know until I talk to Janie."

"Where do you think she is?"

"The hospital, I hope. That's where I left her."

"Is that where you're headed now?"

"No. I'm on my way to the parsonage."

"Why there?"

"That's in case she's not at the hospital."

"Then you'd better get going."

I didn't have to be told twice.

Chapter 23

Jessie was back to being Ms. Hyde. When I turned the ignition key, all I got from her was a high-pitched clatter that set my nerves on edge.

"Damn it, Jessie!"

I got out and using the channel locks that I kept on the front seat for that very purpose, advanced the flywheel a quarter turn. That's all it took. Five minutes later we were at the parsonage.

Leaving Jessie running because she was still as cold as a tomb inside, I went up the steps and through the front door of the parsonage. Literally through the front door. Cecil hadn't left much to chance when he smashed his way inside.

The wind slammed the storm door shut behind me. I reached for the light switch on the wall then thought better of it. I didn't want to attract attention to either myself or my mission.

A quick search of the ground floor told me that no one was there. I went up the stairs and into what I assumed was Janie's bedroom where I discovered a fire-blackened book lying between two throw pillows atop her white bedspread. The book looked like the one I'd seen her carrying out of the church along with the candelabrum. She said it was a Bible, King James version. It turned out to be Janie Hammond's diary.

I stood at the east upstairs window, reading it by street light, when I thought I heard a car start up somewhere below me. But with the wind buffeting the parsonage, it was hard to tell exactly where the car was, whether on the street or in the garage out back. Then I remembered that Jessie had been running the whole time I was in there, which was a sure recipe for disaster.

Taking the diary with me, I went downstairs and was crossing the living room on the way to the back door, when I saw the red light blinking on Janie's answering machine. She had one message. I wondered what it was.

"Mom, this is Michelle. I know you're home, so pick up . . .Mom, answer the phone. Mom? Mom!"

It must have been then that Michelle left her friend's house and started running home. In an effort to do what? Save her mother from suicide? And if so, did Janie really intend to die in the parsonage tonight?

Hours after the fire, the thick smell of smoke still lingered here and would linger for months to come, even after the place had been cleaned top to bottom. Could Janie have sat there in her rocking chair calmly reading her Bible while the smoke crept into her room, then into her nose, into her eyes, and into her lungs? I didn't think so. Then why was she still in the parsonage when Michelle arrived on the scene? She must have forgotten something and gone upstairs after it. Her Bible? No, it was still up in her room on the seat of her rocking chair. Her diary? No, it had been placed carefully on her bed, either to burn in the fire, or more likely, to help her father burn in hell. The only thing that she had seen fit to save from the fire was her ministerial robe. But why it, aside from its intrinsic and symbolic beauty? Surely she didn't plan on ever wearing it again. Or did she?

I ran outside to the garage and found it empty. But the tire tracks in the snow were fresh. The garage hadn't been empty long.

Back in Jessie, I noticed a curious lack of warmth as I headed east on Church Street, then turned south on Fickle Road. Already my breath had frozen on the windshield, and I had to use the ice scraper just to see the road. Last time, Jessie, I vowed. You have failed me for the last time.

Fickle Road was a nightmare. The wind, slicing in from the northwest, cut clouds of snow from the adjoining fields, and there in the flats below Hart's woods, laid a white wall in front of me that seemed to have neither beginning nor end. It mattered not that I could barely see out the windshield for all the frost inside. Once within the wall of white, there was nothing to see. I slowed to a crawl and prayed that no one was headed north on Fickle Road.

I finally found some relief at the bottom of the next hill, when I put a farmhouse and a barn between the wind and me, and then a woods on my way up the next hill. But when I topped the hill and the woods ended, the wind slammed so hard and unexpectedly into Jessie that she began to fishtail back and forth between the two deep ditches that ran on either side of the road. If we slid into either one, I'd never get her out without a wrecker, so I tapped the brakes and again slowed to a crawl.

Once I reached Fickle and turned on County Road J, I stopped long enough to completely clear the windshield inside and out. I didn't need any distractions. From here on in, I had to be absolutely sure of my direction.

Janie's royal blue Buick Regal sat parked at the small public beach there along the east side of Coon Lake. I pulled Jessie up beside it, cut her lights, and killed the engine. Janie wasn't inside the Buick, but all the clothes that she had been wearing earlier that evening were there in the front seat, along with an envelope addressed to "My Darling Michelle." I quietly closed the Buick's door and began to run south along the beach, which I knew would be the route that she would take.

How many times had she rehearsed this? How many times had she gone to the brink and then pulled back, deciding the time wasn't yet right? The dark-haired, dressed-in-white ghost had been Janie; so Michelle hadn't lied to me when she said that her mother was the one who dyed her hair, and not Michelle. Not only dyed it, but cut it before she came back to Oakalla so that no one would recognize her. She never had intended to die in any of the fires that she had set, including the one at the parsonage earlier that night. Her intention all along was to join her father and her sister in the cold black waters of Coon Lake.

I ran through the snow, past darkened cabins and around the sections of piers piled lakeside at the edges of the yards. I could hear waves crash against the shore, and feel their icy spray, which seemed to freeze in the wind before it pelted me. The miracle, it seemed to me, was not that I could run on club-cold feet, but that I would want to.

Fifty yards ahead Janie stood at the edge of the water, waves breaking around her feet. I couldn't tell whether she was facing the lake or facing the shore, or how much time I had to get there.

I slowed to a walk. If she saw me running toward her, she would turn to the lake as she had in the past and simply disappear—this time for all time. Neither did I dare to call out to her, or the same thing would happen. My only hope was that she would be so intent on this, her life's last ritual, that she wouldn't see me coming.

It wasn't to be. When I approached to about 20 yards of her, she went into the water.

Had the wind and waves not been against her, she would have escaped me easily because she was by far the stronger swimmer. But I hit the water on the run, flattened out into a shallow dive, and let my momentum carry me to her. I first grabbed her robe, then her arm as she rolled, and we both went under. I came up coughing but still hanging on. She used her free hand to swing at me, catching me flush in the jaw and filling my head with stars. I grabbed her other arm and under the water we went.

It never occurred to me that I might drown until I felt for the bottom and found none. We'd stepped into a hole, and I, who had little strength left, was now at her mercy.

"Janie, God damn it," I gasped as I turned on my back, trying to keep my head above water. "Do you want to drown us both?"

"Just me," she said, fighting for deep water. "So let go!"

"I won't. Do you hear me? I *won't*."

"You *will*."

She slammed her elbow into my ribs. Still I held on. *She* had to decide she wanted to live. If I made that decision for her, I was only postponing the inevitable.

"Garth, please, I'm not worth dying for."

"I beg to differ."

"You don't mean that."

"Then why am I here?"

She stopped struggling. For an instant I thought that it was a ploy to get me to relax my grip . . . until I felt her start to sob. Or shake. It was damn cold in that water.

Colder yet when we finally dragged ourselves up on shore. But I knew by then that no matter how long and cold the walk back to her car, we would make it.

CHAPTER 24

I sat in the driver's side of Janie's Buick Regal with the motor running, the heat and fan on high, the seat pushed all the way back, and Janie sitting on my lap. It had come to my attention during the past few minutes, whenever I could keep my teeth from chattering, that she wore absolutely nothing under her robe. Likewise, it had no doubt come to her attention what had come to my attention. But she made no offer to move.

"We're going to have a hard time explaining this if somebody comes along," she said between shudders.

"Especially if we die from carbon monoxide poisoning."

"Do you think we should start back to town?"

I checked to see how hard the wind was blowing. Though I could hear it against the car, I no longer saw whitecaps on the lake.

"It might be best if we did start back," I said.

"Are you afraid I might seduce you?"

I eased her off my lap. "You already have."

She let her hand rest lightly on my thigh. "I wish."

"What's the matter?" she said a few seconds later as we still sat there.

"There's something in Jessie I need, but I don't want to go out into the cold again."

"Can't it wait until later?"

"No. I don't think so."

I sprang from the Buick and was back inside it within seconds. But in that short time I began to shake again.

"What was so important that it couldn't wait until tomorrow?"

She sat with her arms folded and her knees locked for warmth, staring at the floor. I dropped her diary at my feet and scooted the seat up over it.

"Something I got for you tonight," I said.

"Before or after the fire?"

"Does it matter?"

Her hand reached out for mine. "No. It doesn't matter."

We had left Coon Lake and the worst of our tremors behind and were on our way east along County Road J when she said, "How much do you know and how much have you guessed?"

"I know very little. I've guessed that your father was molesting you and when you couldn't take it any longer, you killed him then burned his churches later."

"And it's all true. Do you still think I'm worth saving?"

"Yes."

"Why?"

"I'll tell you later. Right now I'd rather know how it all came about, if you're willing to tell me."

"Why wouldn't I be? You saved my life." I felt her shrug. "Whatever that's worth."

"I was at the church the first time it happened."

Janie was speaking. We had just turned on to Fickle Road.

"I was alone there. I was sitting at the front of the sanctuary, when I heard the front door open and the sound of someone's footsteps as they crossed the vestibule. I knew whose they were. I'd heard them come to the door of my bedroom when I was undressing, and to the door of the bathroom when I was taking a bath. I'd heard them in my sleep many times and they always awakened me with a start, a pounding heart, sweaty hands, and throat so dry I couldn't speak. Short, sharp, hard footsteps—I knew in my heart they were evil, and I feared them. So I hid in the closet behind the choir loft. It didn't help. He found me anyway."

A sudden gust of wind shook the Buick. I dropped our speed to 25 to make sure we stayed between the ditches.

"When I was a little girl, he used to spank me with his hand, and those spankings continued long after I thought they should have stopped. But when I told my mother about it, asking for her help, she said I probably deserved them and there wasn't anything she could do about it anyway. So when he began molesting me, I didn't even bother to tell her because I knew she'd just look the other way. But I finally had to tell her because I was going off to college and had my younger sister, Carrie, to think of."

"How long had it been going on by then?"

"Seven years."

"What did your mother say when you told her?"

"She blew up. She called me a slut and a whore and said she didn't have to listen to my filth. And if my father *had* done anything with me, it was because I led him into it. Those were her exact words. It was because *I* led him into it."

Whiteout ahead. I slowed the Buick even more.

Janie said, "You know, the funny thing is that while all of this was going on, my father was treated like a savior everywhere we went. *He* was the one who was going to get the church back on its feet. *He* was the one who was going to build the new educational unit, or the new kitchen. And he was good that way, raising money and bringing people together to build things. And I somehow managed a somewhat normal life. I made good grades, had a lot of friends, including boyfriends, was active in a lot of organizations. To all appearances, I was a normal, even exceptional, kid. But always with this deep dark ugly secret that I could never tell anyone about."

"Maybe that's because you never let him darken your soul. Maybe you still haven't," I said.

"I wish that were true, and thank you for thinking so. But it's not."

"Because of what happened to your sister?"

"Yes."

I waited while she gathered the courage to tell me. We were out of the snow now with only bare road ahead.

"If he hadn't yet, I knew he'd start up with Carrie as soon as I left home. I'd already warned her about him, said that he wasn't the man he appeared to be, but Carrie was one of those trusting people who thought the best of everybody, and wouldn't believe anyone would want to do her harm, especially her own minister-father. Her faith was about to be shattered, along with her life, and I couldn't let that happen because I knew what it was doing to me, and I was the stronger of the two. So in August of that year, just before I was to leave for school, I asked my father if he wouldn't take me fishing one last time for old times' sake."

"You had fished together before?"

"Many times, though not for years. Those were my best memories of us. From early on, I was his fishing buddy and he was mine. So it took me by surprise when he asked Carrie to go along, since he never had before. And even more to my surprise, she, who had never picked up a fishing pole in her life, accepted."

I waited while she composed herself. "This is hard," she said.

"I know."

"It was a hot Sunday afternoon and there were a lot of boats on the water, so I knew that if I could somehow get Carrie out of the way, I might pull it off. But the more I tried to discourage her, the more she insisted that she was going along. Finally I quit arguing with her. It was her life. If she was determined to see it ruined, I couldn't stop her."

"At that point had you given up the idea of killing your father?"

"Yes. I could swim, but he couldn't. Yet he never wore a life jacket, claiming that, as in all other things, the Lord would look after him. But I wouldn't take the chance of drowning him with Carrie in the boat."

"So what happened?"

"What happened was that Carrie decided to stand up and stretch her legs at the same time a ski-boat went past. She lost her balance and tipped us over. At first I couldn't believe it was happening, and then I couldn't believe my good fortune, when I saw my father beating a froth in the water, trying to stay afloat. It never occurred to me that Carrie would try to save him, until she did." The horror of that moment would forever haunt her, no matter where she went from here. "And do you know what that son-of-a-bitch did? He put both arms around her, and then he smiled at me before he took her down. I never saw either one of them again, not even at their funeral. Mother insisted that the caskets be kept closed."

"Why did she do that?"

"For the same reason that she did everything from that day on. To punish me. She knew, or guessed, what had happened. And Carrie was always her favorite."

"So you've been walking the shore ever since, looking for them?"

"Not ever since. I was there a couple times this week, and then a couple times in the past. All I was looking for was some sign that Carrie is all right, that she has passed on and is happy wherever she is. I don't worry about my father. I figure that's between him and God."

I felt my nape start to tingle, but knew that there was no one in the back seat watching me. "You haven't been putting in regular appearances there at the cabin over the years?" I said.

"No. What would be the point, except to torture myself?"

"Was Carrie's hair long and dark like Michelle's?"

"Yes. They could have passed for sisters. We all could have at that age."

The tingling went away. Somehow there was a logical explanation, but it wasn't up to me to find it.

"What was the last straw? Was it your divorce?" I said.

"Yes. I had finally put everything behind me, or so I thought, and had what I believed was a pretty good life, when out of the blue Bill said that he wanted a divorce, that he'd found someone else, the soul mate he'd been searching for all of his life. It turned out that she was really his old flame from college, recently widowed.

They hooked up again when he went back for his 40th reunion."

We were coming into Oakalla. It was a welcome sight.

"Were you having problems in your marriage?" I said.

"No more than most, I didn't think. But maybe in my attempt to be normal, I'd become dull." She smiled. "Remember? Wild Bill never took many prisoners."

I thought of all of the rejoinders that I could offer in her defense, but kept my peace. Diana Baldwin had once loved me with all of her heart, as I had once loved her with all of mine. She still loved me, I believed, but a month ago today she had married a rancher from New Mexico. So how could any of us, who had fought the wars and lost most of them, make sense out of it all?

I parked her Buick in front of the shelter and left the motor running. To my relief, I saw a light on in the shelter and someone standing in the front window. It looked a whole lot like Ruth.

"Which church did you start with?" I said.

"I didn't start with a church. I started with our cabin. I drove out there with an empty two-gallon can of gas in the trunk of my car, thinking that if it were meant to be, I'd find a way. I did find a way, by going down the coal chute in Fickle Store and then turning on the gas pumps. My heart was going about 200 miles an hour the whole time I was there, but it gave me such a rush, the rest was easy. And as sick as it sounds, I've never been more alive than on the nights of the fires."

"When did Michelle become involved?"

"She never became involved. But when I cut and dyed my hair right before we moved to Oakalla, she called me on it." Involuntarily she reached up to touch the hair that was no longer there. "Then she couldn't understand why we needed three gas cans and why I always kept all three full."

We didn't speak for a while. I was satisfied to sit there with my arm around her. She was satisfied to sit there and be held. And with Ruth waiting there inside the shelter, it almost felt like a first date.

"So Michelle was on to you from the time you arrived in Oakalla?" I said.

"Let's just say I'd created some questions in her mind. Then the night I burned down Fickle Store, when I thought that she was sound asleep, she met me at the door and asked me where I'd been."

"Had the fire siren rung yet?"

"No. She had to be awake when I left."

"What did you tell her?"

"I told her I had a date. But I don't think she believed me."

"Who was the lucky guy?"

She looked up at me and smiled. "You were, as a matter of fact. I knew she'd approve."

We sat some more without saying anything. It was hard to get it in my head that this likely would be our last sitting. She had so much to offer and yet so much to overcome.

She said, "But the night that I set fire to the church, I know that Michelle saw me either going or coming. That's why she lied to you and said that she'd seen a man leaving the church. She couldn't believe that I would do such a thing; yet she had to believe her own eyes."

"Which was why she kept such a close eye on you after that?"

She nodded. "Michelle was convinced by my actions that I had some kind of death wish. Since she didn't know my reasons, it was the only logical conclusion."

"Or maybe she saw it as the only logical conclusion, period. She's a very bright girl, remember?"

"She takes after her father in that respect."

"She takes after both her parents."

She touched her hand to mine then quickly withdrew it. "Thank you for that, Garth. But I know what I am."

"Which is?"

"A failure. I've failed as a daughter, as a sister, as a wife, and, which hurts the most, as a minister. And I don't need to look out at my yawning, dwindling congregation. My own daughter tells me that."

"You haven't failed as a mother."

"Yes. But what's a *mother* to do with her life to make a living?"

"A lot of things. Preaching just doesn't happen to be one of them."

"Et tu, Brute."

"I couldn't do it either. I have to respect those who can."

"But my father, for all his black-hearted sins, could. So could Wild Bill, who gunned down a man on the highway. Why can't I?"

256

"Why can't I sing or paint or play the piano, or do a dozen other things I'd love to be able to do? We can't will our true self. We have to find it. Sometimes that takes a heap of looking."

"And if we never find our true self? Remember, I'm pushing 45."

"You will. With God's help."

For the second time that night she elbowed me in the ribs. But this one was a lot gentler. "How can you say that? You aren't sure you even believe in God."

"But you do. That's all that matters."

We sat for a while longer. She said, "I guess I'd better go inside." Then she kissed me. It was perhaps the sweetest, most tender kiss of my life. "Goodbye, Garth. Stay well."

I opened the door and climbed out. After I'd helped her out, I reached under the seat and handed the blackened diary to her.

"You asked me what I had to offer in your defense," I said. "Here it is, in your own words. It's the girl you used to be."

She gingerly took the diary from me as if it were fine china, as if dropped, it might shatter.

"My grandmother gave me this for my 10th birthday. I faithfully wrote in it every day after that. I was writing in it that day in the church when I heard his footsteps. I remember hiding it under a stack of hymnals in the closet and then not finding it again until this week. I intended to keep it all of my life, but after that day at the church,

I never wrote in it again." She balled her hands into fists, as tears streamed down her cheeks. "My God, what that man took from me!"

"Hold that thought. It might help you through this."

I glanced up to see that Ruth was back at the window. I could leave Janie here, knowing that she was in the best possible hands.

"You'd better get inside," I said. "Before we both freeze."

But she wasn't listening. "You *do* think I'm worth it, don't you?"

"It doesn't matter what I think." I patted the diary. "Read this. Then ask her what she thinks."

I walked her up the seven concrete steps to the front door of the shelter. When she was safely inside, I went home.

CHAPTER 25

Eight days had passed. Thanksgiving had come and gone.

Michelle was out of the hospital and living with her father and her stepmother in DeLand, Florida. Janie had been released on her own recognizance while awaiting trial and was living with a friend of the family in Madison, where she was undergoing counseling.

At Janie's request I had not tried to see her in the interim. She wanted to be a whole person, she said, before we next met, which she also said, might be a while. I held no great hope for Janie and me because I already had a whole woman in the person of Abby Airhart. If I had to wait for someone, it would be Abby.

Hattie Peeler had walked all the way to my office in the face of a cold west wind to tell me that she'd received a phone call from Camelia that very morning, and while Camelia had not said where she was, only that it was very cold and snowy there, she was doing well. She expected to see Hattie again one of these days, but she would make no promises.

Larry Don Loomus' body had been flown back to Isabella County, Mississippi, and he was buried in the Loomus family cemetery there on his cattle ranch. I had yet to hear from Stonewall Jackson Huff on the fate of Orion. But my gut feeling was that he would beat any and all charges against him and continue to thrive as the guru of asceticism—until he self-destructed, as all self-appointed messiahs seem to do.

Having finally received his insurance money from the fire, Jasper Peterson had immediately disappeared, leaving his house unsold and the eyesore that was once Fickle Store for someone else to clean up. His sudden disappearance left Ruth and me to wonder about Jasper's first fire, if perhaps Carl Bolin wasn't right in his assertion that Jasper was responsible.

And now that Old Elmo's head was hanging in Beezer's cabin, the local deer hunters had lost interest in trespassing on Beezer's property, and he was getting a lot more reading done of late. He'd offered me some of his books to "hold me over winter," but so far I hadn't taken him up on it.

As for me, I was out walking Daisy on this cold, still Sunday morning following Thanksgiving. Most of the snow from the previous week had melted in an all-day rain before the cold had set in again, so Delpha Wright was out raking and burning the last of her leaves. I stood a while watching her, before catching a whiff of smoke that transported me back to childhood.

Nothing like the smell of burning leaves to remind me of how fall once tasted; of Jack Frost, hayrides, snow flakes on the tip of my tongue, leaf piles that never got burned because we were too busy diving into them, and one-man games of football played between the Chinese elm and the rose of Sharon bush in our back yard; that it's often a long lonely walk from our expectations of life to its reality.

Daisy and I went on south to the United Methodist Church, which was locked, its windows boarded, as we, its members, decided its fate. Already I knew how the vote would go. Over my protest we would relocate west of town, where we would build a new church and educational unit. There in the middle of Emmett Milner's corn field we would have all the room for parking we now lacked, plus all the room to expand we would never need.

What could I say in the old church's defense? Nothing that would make either economic or logistical sense, so there was little point in saying it. My loyalty was to the building itself, the people who had worshiped there and the memories we had made, not to the abstraction, the body of the risen Christ, its present congregation. My grief was for its bricks and mortar, chapel, sanctuary, and bell tower, its rugged cross and old-time religion, those bulwarks that had held fast against the sea change within me and led me to calmer, safer waters.

At issue was its resurrection from the fire, and there

I stood on the forecastle saying we should all go down with the ship. It was not a popular position. Neither was it a sane one.

I heard church bells. Daisy whined and gave a tug on her leash, as if to say it was time to move on. I agreed. So on we walked, along that sleeping city sidewalk— the sound of Sunday morning coming down.

About the Author

John R. Riggs is a husband, father, grandfather, walker of dogs, and builder of fires. He lives with his wife Carole on a small farm near Greencastle, Indiana, where he keeps busy doing all the things country life requires.

Throughout the years he has worked as a teacher, football coach, quality control foreman, and carpenter. He was crew chief for James R. Gammon in Gammon's landmark research on the Wabash River. Presently, as he has done for the past 30 years, he works as a researcher for DePauw University Archives. He also mixes chemicals for Co-Alliance, Bainbridge, Indiana. And he writes.

He is the author of 13 books in the Garth Ryland mystery series and has been praised by the New York Times as "a writer with real imagination."